THE FIELD OF JUSTICE

THE FIELD OF JUSTICE

Moonshine and Murder in North Georgia

William A. Thomas, Jr.

GREEN ALTAR BOOKS
SHOTWELL PUBLISHING

Produced in the Republic of South Carolina by

Green Altar Books, an imprint of Shotwell Publishing LLC

Post Office Box 2592

Columbia, South Carolina 29202

www.ShotwellPublishing.com

Cover Design by Boo Jackson

ISBN: 978-1-963506-07-5

FIRST EDITION

10 9 8 7 6 5 4 3 2 1

CONTENTS

For Jerry A. Taylor

Author's Note

In September of 2020, as I talked with my aunt, Gillian Thomas Tilghman, about the then-recent release of my first book *Runaway Haley*, she asked what my next story might be about and when I would begin work on it. Since that book had been about my wife's family, I thought that I should write about something from my own family's history. This book is an account of the events in the life of one of my paternal great-great-great-grandfathers. While our family's oral history had already characterized James Bennett Godard for me, genealogical and newspaper records available on-line added a fascinating new wrinkle to the story that I had not heard before, and I wanted to know more about him. Eventually, I made contact with Mr. Jerry Taylor, a historian who knew a great deal about my ancestor, and he gave me some tremendous resources that led to the story you are about to read.

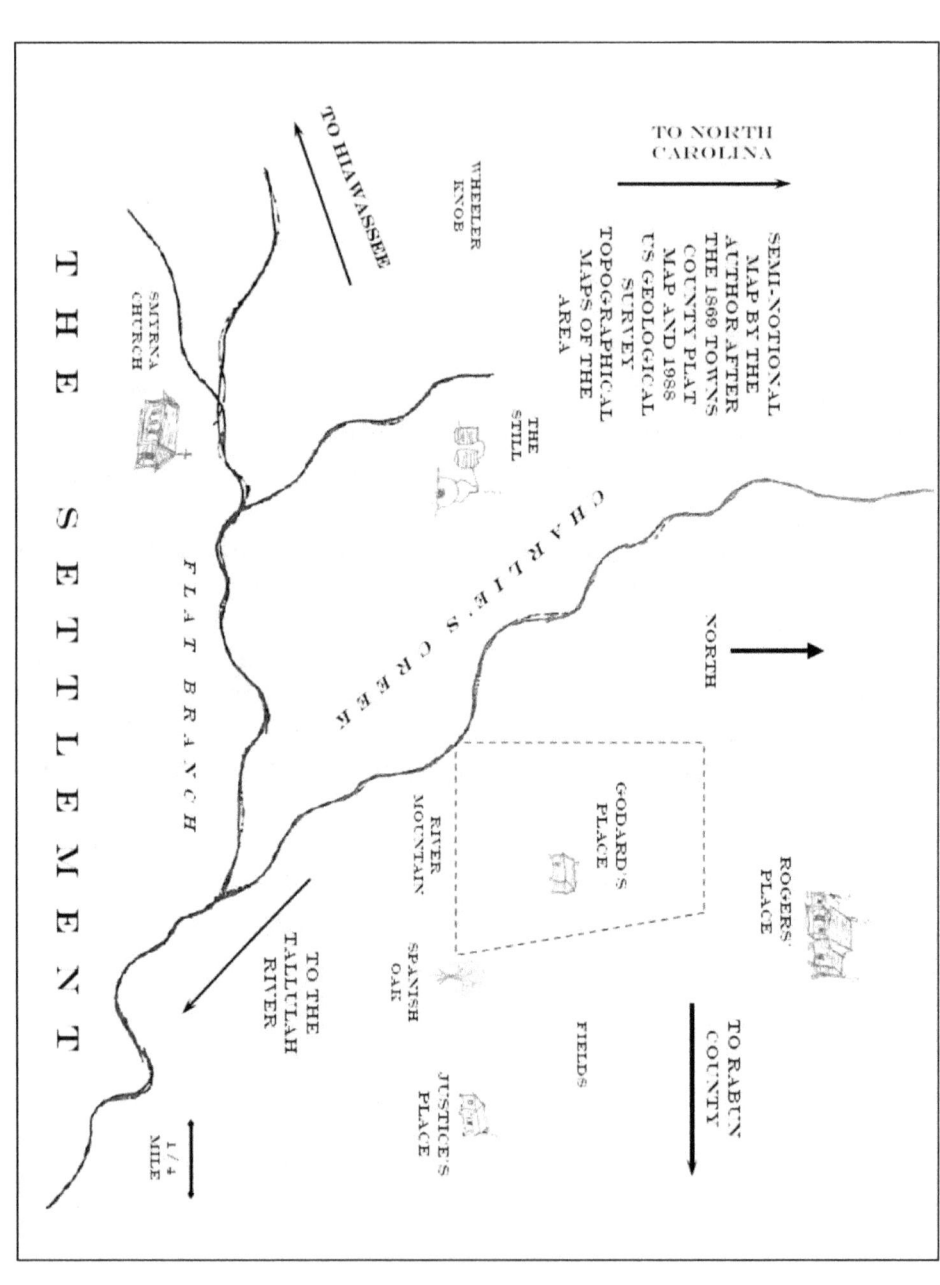

THE SETTLEMENT

SEMI-NOTIONAL MAP BY THE AUTHOR AFTER THE 1869 TOWNS COUNTY PLAT MAP AND 1988 US GEOLOGICAL SURVEY TOPOGRAPHICAL MAPS OF THE AREA

TO NORTH CAROLINA

TO HIAWASSEE

WHEELER KNOB

SMYRNA CHURCH

THE STILL

CHARLIE'S CREEK

FLAT BRANCH

NORTH

GODARD'S PLACE

ROGERS' PLACE

RIVER MOUNTAIN

TO RABUN COUNTY

TO THE TALLULAH RIVER

SPANISH OAK

FIELDS

JUSTICE'S PLACE

1/4 MILE

Chapter One

———— • ————

November 18, 1887: A Cautionary Tale

R osa Nicholson was only six—she couldn't know that when she was very old, she would recount this day's events to her grandchildren.

Like any other morning in their cabin on the remote farm in the southern Appalachian Mountains, she awakened to hear her mother and brothers in the room below. She got up and changed from her night clothes into a simple cotton dress made from an old skirt and came down the ladder from the loft in her sock feet for breakfast with her younger brother, Benjamin. Always the same porridge. Her father, Absalom, came in from the barn with her oldest brother Andrew following behind. They already had been up for an hour or more getting the chores done.

"Eat up. We're all ready to go," Absalom said, removing his hat and hanging his coat on the peg. "Wagon's loaded."

Rosa's mother sighed and shook her head silently. When they were all finally ready, her father hoisted Rosa into the back of the wagon and tucked the quilt around her as she wriggled in among the bushel baskets and bags of apples with Benjamin. Andrew rode on the seat with their mother, who held baby Samuel.

"Daddy, I want to ride on the bench, too," she said, sticking out her lip with a pout. Her father had, not infrequently, changed his mind about something when she'd done that before. This time, though, he didn't relent.

"Naw baby girl, it'll be warmer down here out of the wind, I promise. You sit tight." He smiled and pinched her cheek playfully. A late November chill had settled over the North Georgia mountains during the preceding week after an initial very cold snap, then a re-warming earlier in the month. The first frost had brought a dusting of snow to the peak of the Brasstown Bald. The old-timers predicted a hard winter.

"You'n help me sell more of them apples today, an' we might could get us a treat in town before we come home," he said, smiling as he stepped up into the driver's seat next to his wife.

"Can't you just go?" asked Virginia, turning to her husband. "I don't even want to think about it."

"Preacher said it keeps folks on the Godly way."

Are we going to church today? thought Rosa. She noticed that her mother wore her regular dress, not the Sunday one.

"Children shouldn't have no part of this if you ask me," said Virginia.

"Samuel's too young to remember anythin' now. Stay at the back, an' you can keep Ben and Rosa distracted."

Virginia pulled the quilt tighter around herself and baby Samuel as they started off north toward town an hour away—rumbling over jarring ruts until they reached the more traveled roads coming down from the hills of Fodder Creek, past Macedonia, and on toward Hiawassee. Flame-brilliant red and yellow trees lined the roads. Their leaves shimmered in the sun, colored by the cold snap, but not yet weak enough to fall.

At the edge of town, wagons and foot traffic filled the usually wide-open streets as they would again for the Saturday markets the next day. A different feeling filled the air today, though. Rosa stared out over the side of the wagon bed, excited and curious to see so many people. Absalom maneuvered the horses to park the wagon along a raised board sidewalk across the street from the courthouse, and he got down from the driver's seat with Andrew after setting the brake. Down the hill beyond the courthouse, toward the creek, a crowd gathered with a carnival-like atmosphere. Rosa had never seen so many people in one place—not even at the church picnic.

"Papa, what's that down there?" She pointed down to the mass of people crowding the stage below. She noticed the disagreeable look that her mother gave him as he let down the side of the wagon facing the walkway to access the baskets of apples.

"Nothin' but some hungry folks who need'n some apples to take home this afternoon. You an' your ma' stay here and see how many you can sell. Andrew, come on wi' me." Ab kissed his wife on the cheek. "We'll be back directly," he said, guiding Andrew behind the wagon to cross the street and head down into the crowd. "Don't worry."

"Where's Papa going?" asked Ben, who was just three. He stood up in the back of the wagon.

"He'll be right back, don't worry," said Virginia, with a cheerful and reassuring tone that didn't match the look on her face.

For the next hour, Rosa sat in the wagon with Ben and played with baby Samuel and her doll while her mother sold apples to passers-by at two-for-a-nickel or a dozen-for-a-quarter. Her ma joked and laughed with her grown-up friends and acquaintances, some of whom Rosa recognized from church, but many of the greetings were followed by subdued murmurings as the ladies huddled together with serious faces and words not meant for children to hear.

Rosa climbed onto the wagon bench and stood, looking down the hill over the congregation at the stage in the center, newly built and bright with the freshness of the wood. The people seemed to press in closer as three men climbed the stairs.

Rosa looked around at her mother, still talking with the church ladies, and then down to her brothers, asleep on the empty fruit bags. She wanted to ask questions, but she knew she shouldn't interrupt the grown-ups. The crowd below paused and grew quiet, but her mother and the others talked on—more audible now to Rosa.

"Did you see his wife today?"

"No, did you?"

"No. I don't know if I could come, but I s'pose she has to."

"Just awful. Met her once in town—nice enough. Such a pity. Don' know how they'll get along now, an' kids to feed."

"They gon' move away, I 'spect. Had to sell."

Down below, near the creek, Rosa watched the men on the stage. The man with the Bible and the dark suit wasn't the preacher from their church. He was younger than her father, but he looked tired. His shoulders slumped in a sad way as he stood at the center of the platform, looking up the hill to survey all the people who stood, now silent, watching him. Another man brought a chair; then the Bible man sat down. He caressed the unopened book on his lap. The congregation waited.

Eventually, he spoke.

"This day been long comin'. It'll be hard, but you gotta know what happens here is part of God's plan." He took a long pause and looked around. "You'n all quote th' verse on th' wages of sin—you know it, an' so do I. Ever'body's a sinner here," he waved his hand out over the gathering, "but none so great as me, that's fer sure." He clutched his fist over his heart, then pointed into the crowd, motioning to a woman there. She handed a little baby up to the stage, and he sat it on his lap, kissed it on the forehead, and stared at the child for a moment. Muffled sobs came from some of the women. Rosa turned and looked over at her mother, who pressed a handkerchief to her eyes and bit her lip.

The man looked out into the crowd and raised his voice. "This child is innocent now, but he'll grow up to be jus' like me and jus' like you—a sinner. All us is."

Rosa sensed that this wasn't like regular church, not just that they were outside. There, most folks were cheerful, but today everyone looked so serious that it made her wary.

The Bible man continued. "But God can forgive. We're all guilty of murder—we killed Jesus. Our sins caused Him to die. If we hadn'a sinned, Jesus wouldn'a had t' go to th' cross—but we're all sinners, an' He died for us. Make yer choice. Yer day's comin', too. Do it sooner'n I did. Choose Jesus and choose right."

He handed the Bible to the man next to him and stood, balancing the baby on his hip. He turned his back to the crowd and nodded slowly.

At the top of the hill, just near where she stood on the front bench of her family's wagon, Rosa saw two men on the other side of the road. The taller man reached into the back of another wagon and pulled a shotgun from under some blankets. He checked it, cocked it, then nodded. The other man turned to face the stage below and signaled with a raised arm.

On the platform, they'd hung a rope over a cross piece with a loop tied on the end. It reminded Rosa of the swing that her daddy had made for them in one of the big trees at the farm, but suddenly, she felt scared and wished that she was home now.

Where's Papa? She searched the crowd below for her father and brother.

The men helped the Bible man walk unsteadily to the center of the platform, then turned him around to face the congregants. Tears streamed down his face as they put a black hood over his head and peeled the crying baby from his arm, passing the infant back down into the crowd. They tied the man's hand to his belt and put the loop of rope over his head, cinching it tightly around his neck.

Why are they doin' that to him? What's happening? Rosa watched the man at the nearby wagon raise the gun, pointing the barrel into the air; then she looked beyond him, down over the silent and still crowd transfixed by the scene before them.

He pulled the trigger.

When the gun fired, the mass of people below flinched as though it was one being, and Rosa saw the pale dots of individual faces as the onlookers gasped and turned in unison—startled by the shot behind them, suddenly distracted from the passion on the stage before them, the crowd looked back up the hill to see what had just happened.

A single voice from the platform broke the brief silence. "I love you, Annie!"

With a heaving motion, one of the men pulled a lever, and the hooded Bible man fell through the floor. He stopped instantaneously— halfway to the ground—and made violent, jerking spasms. Once, twice, three times. Still.

The faces turned back to the scene on the platform just as a woman near the front let out a long, low wail. Children cried. A buzzing murmur swept across the gathering when they saw the body—dangling below the floor, head cocked to one side at a grotesque angle, a big knot of rope at its ear.

Suddenly, Rosa felt herself being yanked down from the wagon bench and spun around. Arms wrapped around her head, burying her face into her mother's coarse apron.

"It'll be all right, honey," she rocked gently. "Ever'thin's gon' be all right."

Rosa pulled free and looked up at her mother.

"What happened? Why did they do that?" Fear washed over her.

Virginia shook her head slightly, pursed her lips, and pulled her in close again—both of them trembling.

"Thou shalt not kill."

While they waited for her father and brother to return, Virginia continued to sell the apples to whoever would buy, but she made Rosa sit on the side of the boardwalk so that the horses and wagon blocked much of her view. Nevertheless, she sneaked peeks at every opportunity, catching glimpses of the scene below.

After several minutes, someone mounted the steps with a knife and cut the rope while another held the dangling legs, and the body collapsed onto his shoulder. They laid it in a coffin to remove the rope and the hood as somber men in dark clothes inspected it for several minutes. On the platform, someone cut the rope into short lengths, unwound the cords, and threw them out to the onlookers clamoring for a souvenir.

"Here! Over here!"

"Gimme one, too!"

A few lucky townspeople held their prizes aloft with joyful grins, and others gathered around the body to gawk at the gruesome sight.

Back down toward the river, a group of ladies huddled around a woman in a black dress who leaned against a tree and sobbed. She held the baby.

When the crowd finally thinned, a small group covered the coffin and loaded it into a wagon; then a mule pulled from the front while the menfolk pushed as they started up from the creek. The black-clad woman followed, supported by two others with more crying children in tow. Mournful sounds of a few singing voices floated in the air, growing louder as they approached, then breaking from unison into a tinny, two-part harmony.

I saw a way-worn traveler,
in tattered garments clad,

And struggling up the mountain,
it seemed that he was sad;

His back was laden heavy; his
strength was almost gone,

Yet he shouted as he journeyed,
"Deliverance will come!"

Then palms of victory, crowns of glory,

Palms of victory I shall wear.

Chapter Two

◄►——— • ———◄►

SATURDAY, NOVEMBER 6, 1886

As the sun peeked over the knob to let a weak late-autumn light down into the Blue Ridge Gap, the waters of the Flat Branch released early morning breath to the cold air and started the journey east. The branch flowed downward, twisting along the sides of the hills, and gurgling through an open area known to locals as "The Settlement," where the branch actually was flat and where the community's tiny Smyrna Church had views onto the widely scattered cabins dotting the surrounding mountains. The branch was wider and more shallow there, not even ankle deep in the places where rocks pushed up from the bottom to break its surface as steppingstones, but it ran deeper in the curves tucked under the mountain laurels, hiding snakes and frogs in the warmer months. Wider and faster, it made its descent to join Charlie's Creek, which then carved its way south through the canyon to meet the upper waters of the Tallulah River in the far northeast of Georgia. Just a generation ago, this had been Cherokee country, and it was still a wilderness.

The Settlement had nothing to draw people to it, save an opportunity for land and the prospect of an isolated life in poverty. Families named Eller, Shook, Burrell, Nicholson, Seay, Arrowood, Garret, Spivy, and Walls lived scattered across the hills in an insular world, marrying among themselves and working to support their families. Fewer than a hundred people lived within walking distance of the Smyrna Church—and nearly everyone had to walk. Horses were few, and a wagon couldn't navigate the narrow and often steep paths to the cabins of the hardscrabble occupants. The occasional open space had been made arable only through years of hard work but still required preparation, diligence, and patient attention to coax food from the earth. Nothing was ever wasted. No one there had anything to speak of, but what they did have was readily shared—labor, resources, knowledge. Overall, though, the people seemed happy, for the most part.

Halfway up on River Mountain, which guarded the confluence of the Flat Branch and Charlie's Creek, Tilmon Justice awoke to the brightening of the single pane of thick, wavy glass in the only window of a two-room cabin. He squinted and grimaced through the headache and the cobwebs, then, wiping his hand across his parched mouth, he struggled to sit and saw the puffs of his breath in the morning light. The fire had gone out in the front room. Annie lay motionless, still asleep under the quilts. He rubbed her back with the stub of his left arm as he sat up.

"Gotta git some firewood."

Steadying himself with his one hand against the wall, he took a couple of wide-legged steps to the table in the front room and poured a glass of water from the metal pitcher, finishing it in four gulps.

Too much, he thought, *shouldn'a drunk so much.*

More and more often he'd had that remorseful thought in the morning, but he liked the way the corn made him feel at the time, offering a temporary escape from his worries and cares. The next day though, the morning was bad, and the troubles were all still waiting on him.

Tilmon sat for a moment. Other than the table and several chairs, only a larder and a small pot belly stove furnished the front room. The two-room cabin sat sideways on a small, flat shoulder nearly halfway up River Mountain, set above the ground on carefully stacked piles of flat stones, with long hand-hewn logs chinked with manure and mud. The exterior wood was darkening up now after six years, and the floors were wearing smooth from footsteps and Annie's sweeping and scrubbing. The door faced the morning sun, allowing for shade on the front porch in the afternoons, while the window in the back room faced south and swung out to let the air through. The house didn't smell like new wood anymore. It smelled like home—a familiar combination of cooking and children and dogs and sweat and the corn.

Five-year-old Isaac and his little sister Lura slept in a pile of blankets on the floor near the fireplace, but the empty space in the corner by the stove caught his eye, and, for a just moment, Tilmon wondered where Silas was. Then he remembered.

He stepped into his pants and worked the suspenders over his shoulders, not buttoning the flap, then pulled on a coat and struggled into the boots, which were still not fully broken in. Squinting as he opened the door to step outside, he retrieved a short, corked bottle from its hiding place in the eaves on the front porch and walked out into the yard. He leaned against an old tree and pissed in the fallen leaves.

A cauldron pot, tools, toys, and junk littered the yard around a spot where an open fire burned much of the time. It was out here, in the yard and on the porch, that most all the family's existence played out—the daily chores, the boredom and the worry, the bickering, the hunger, and a few good times with the corn. Down the hill, he had a shed for his farm tools and for the mare. Next to it sat a small smokehouse that didn't get much use since they didn't have livestock, and he wasn't a good hunter. Tilmon's fields lay to the northwest, below those of his nearest neighbor, a half a mile away.

This morning's headache was a leftover from the celebration after completing the plowing and planting. Tilmon didn't ever need too much of a special occasion to have a drink—he took to the corn nearly every day. Most nights, he sat outside around the fire with whoever stopped by and passed around the jars and bottles he had, or whatever his friends brought with them. Often though, he sat alone with the corn for no real reason at all. But finishing the planting—now that was something of an accomplishment, and it deserved a bit more, he thought.

Tilmon and Silas had been working the upper field for winter wheat. He was tired of just cornbread and was looking forward to Annie baking a real loaf of bread after the harvest. Maybe even a pie crust. Weeks ago, they took the swing blade to the whole hill, then had the mare pull a rake plow across and back so the furrows would catch the rain and not run off with the dirt and seeds. They cleared debris just like he'd done for the past three years—setting rocks to the side for later use and chopping out roots and sticks to burn. Each year the task became a little less onerous, and the field got a little better. They had to wait for his wife to tell them when the signs were right before they scattered the wheat.

Tilmon didn't believe much in the signs, but Annie swore by them. Depending on the phase of the moon and where it was in the star signs each month, she determined what she would do herself at the house and what she would tell him was good to do on that day. He couldn't make much sense of it. She said that certain days of the month were the best days for cutting your hair: when the signs were in the kidneys, the thighs, the legs, or the feet. *Seems like you'd cut your hair when the signs were in the head*, he thought, but Annie said that was the time for baking and cooking. Some days were good for setting apart eggs for hatching, others for planting or harvesting. Even putting shingles on the house had to be done when the signs were right for it. When they first commenced to building the cabin, Annie had talked to her kinfolk about when to start out with laying the foundation stones. This week, she'd said that the moon was in the eighth sign, the loins—with two of the best days of the month for planting crops that bear above ground—so she told Tilmon and Silas to put down the wheat then.

On the western side of the upper field, up a small rise, his nearest neighbor had watched their labors every day in silence.

Tilmon took two big swigs of relief from the bottle and stared at the end of his left arm where his hand should have been. The limb stopped abruptly as a fleshy, calloused knob just below the elbow. He'd never had a left hand, so he didn't know to miss it, but he thought sometimes about how its absence had shaped and challenged his whole life. Taunting from other kids hadn't been a problem. As the baby, his eight older siblings had protected him well—so much so that he'd always had to prove to them that he was able enough instead of letting them do for him. Just after his twentieth birthday, he left Rabun County to come to live at Charlie's Creek and make a life for himself. It was a surprise to his family, but he was determined, and he told them that he had it to do. The Settlement community here had been pretty good to him over the past decade. Mr. Rogers took him on for work and let him live at their place, and when he and Rogers' niece Annie had announced to marry, a dozen men spent almost a whole week building their cabin with him. The piece of land had been Rogers', and he sold Tilmon the parcel for a good price. They'd gone down to the courthouse to tell the sale to the clerk who wrote it in the record book and had each of them make their mark, but no money changed hands that day. Every month, Tilmon was supposed to pay some to Rogers, but most often he couldn't—and that was OK. Annie was family, and they weren't going anywhere.

Like everyone else here, they had nothing to start with and had to build or make or grow everything they needed—but for all his efforts, the place couldn't support more crops than just getting by even when he did have help to work the fields. After Isaac's birth, Tilmon knew he had to do more to provide. It was then that he started in the corn business.

He took another swig and stretched as his fog lifted, then went back inside with a small load of sticks tucked under his left arm and a single log in his hand. Everyone was still asleep. Tilmon fed the fire and made a lunch pail from the larder but left most of the little they had for his kids. He put on his leather sash as he grabbed his things to head out.

It took ten minutes to walk the quarter mile down the southern slope of River Mountain where he met the trail to the branch. At the bottom, he turned west and continued upstream, then walked that much further again to pass the Smyrna Church. He continued upward from there, following a main tributary of the branch while stepping back and forth across the water at intervals to make his way higher, up toward Wheeler Knob. There wasn't really a trail, and Tilmon didn't want one. He tried to vary his route up the hill each time he went—part of the effort to keep the place secluded and not leave signs—but if somebody really wanted to know where his operation was, they didn't have to look too hard. It wasn't far to where he was going, just about two miles, but the terrain and his efforts at keeping out of sight and not leaving signs meant that it took nearly three-quarters of an hour to get there most days.

Even though he was new to the business compared to most, Tilmon had quickly developed a reputation for a good product over the past year. After working and watching other stillers for a few years, listening and learning, he'd figured out enough to try to make a go of it on his own. He couldn't have built the rig by himself, but even with folks to help, it hadn't been easy. Since right after the war started, the government wanted to tax the production of liquor, and the federals would pay ten dollars to someone for rattin' out a stiller. If you got caught, you'd get a fine, your rig would get busted up, and all of your liquor would get poured out on the spot. Everything had to be done in secret.

The stream got narrower and ran a little faster as the sides of the cove grew steep. It originated in a little spring at its highest point, above where he was headed, and the tributaries and little rivulets of runoff added in here and there. When he reached the dense clump of evergreen mountain laurels that obscured the way forward, Tilmon ducked in under the leaves of the lowest limbs. He grabbed a tree trunk for support and climbed up four steppingstones into the wide, flat opening carved out of the middle of the thicket.

The clearing was easily five times larger than his cabin, bounded on all sides by the dense foliage. Inside, the high walls of the thicket amplified the sound of the stream, invisible behind a tall growth of weeds on the far side of the clearing. The thick laurel bushes gave a heavy, sweet fragrance when they flowered in the early summer, when the whole place hummed with the buzz of the bees. Today though, all you could smell was the putrid-sweet smell of the mash. Opposite the branch, they had set up their rig with a pile of firewood nearby. Beyond that were strewn random parts and pieces, and a tiny shack where they kept supplies and slept—guarding the place and tending the mash that bubbled below ground in the half-buried barrels.

Chapter Three

SATURDAY, NOVEMBER 6, 1886

One of Tilmon's connections knew a man from over in Rabun named Jason Coward. He had a son who was sort of touched in the head and needed to get out of the house for some work. They figured he'd do all right at this job if you told him exactly what to do and didn't expect him to think too much for himself. Tilmon knew how it felt to be young and on his own with some disadvantage, so he took him on. Silas had been staying with them for several weeks now. He served as Tilmon's extra hand and was gradually becoming more comfortable with the Justice family.

Tilmon called out as he approached the tiny wooden shack. "Silas! Get up! Gonna start the run today." When he opened the door, he found Silas already awake, sitting on the side of the cot and pulling on his boots. Silas was just eighteen. Tall and lanky. He looked just about like any other kid from up here in the mountains—what with his too-short pants held up by a belt of braided strips of colored cloth and a shirt that was well-worn by others before it got to him. It was when he opened his mouth, though, that you noticed two things. First, his teeth: missing, misshapen, miscolored, and misaligned. Then, if he could get any words out at all, you'd wonder why he would say such a thing. Most often though, he appeared ready to speak, but no words came.

Silas wiped his chin with the back of his hand and grinned. "Hey, Mr. Justice," he said in his odd, slow way.

"G'morning, Silas. All ready?" Tilmon handed over the food pail. He lifted the top of the nearest barrel, and the pungent sour-sweet smell assaulted his nose. The cap of ground corn debris that had been floating on top of the mixture at first had now sunk into the barrel, revealing a yellowish broth with stray pieces of meal floating in it.

A month before, they'd pulled out a meat grinder and clamped it to the edge of the table in the shed to grind the dried, sprouted corn by the hand full. Sprouting in colder weather was a lot of work. They had warmed the white corn kernels in big wash tubs by the stove in his cabin, rinsing and draining and mixing them every morning until they grew worm-like roots nearly as long as a man's thumb, then set them out to dry. Summertime sprouting was easier—just a thick layer of wet corn in big sacks set out to bake in the sun under a layer of hay and manure. The grinder rocked on the edge of the table, making difficult work for a one-armed man. It would have been easier to have the grinding done at a mill—one with a stone turned by a horse or by a water wheel. There was a couple of those around, but when he asked his wife's uncle to use the one they had down below their house, the answer was no.

Dang it, Rogers. Illegal to grind sprout—ha! Illegal don't keep him from drinkin' and near about everything else about the likker business.

The sprouted corn, thus dried and ground, was malt. They heated the pure, clear water from the branch in a big cauldron to hot-but-not-boiling, then added four times as much ground corn and kept it moving in the pot with a big paddle. When it cooled a bit, they added one part malt and cooked it a bit more. Eventually, they squeezed the corn down and took off as much of the cloudy yellow mash as they could get, pouring it into the barrels in the floor of the shed. The liquid fermented for two or three weeks until it became a murky, pungent beer; then they strained it again and distilled it in the copper rig to make the sparkling, clear moonshine. If Tilmon had the time and inclination, and if there was enough volume, he could distill the moonshine a second time to double the alcohol content and increase the selling price.

Tilmon tasted the mash beer. He puckered his lips and squeezed his eyes shut. "Pretty good flavor. Let's fire it up and get goin'. You scrub out the still good?"

"Yessir. Washed it out four times, like you said. Clean and shiny."

"Gotta be real clean. Dirty likker'll make yer head pound for sure."

Tilmon went back outside to inspect the setup that had taken them weeks to build. Over the past year, he'd collected supplies from over in Rabun and down Hiawassee and had parts crafted by experts in the trade from up in North Carolina, all of which were then smuggled into the hiding place in disguise or under cover of night. He was still having to pay them back for the pieces, and they took their fees in cash and liquor. The groundhog furnace was a twelve-foot-long rectangular pit dug into the earth and reinforced at the mouth of the firebox and along the inside walls with rock. The roof of the furnace was covered with flat rocks and sealed tight with multiple layers of clay, baked hard by the heat. A fifty-gallon copper still sat down in the pit on an earthen shelf behind the firebox. It was a round-bottom cauldron, half sticking up through the roof of the groundhog pit, with a tight neck at the top. A slop-arm drain ran out from the side of the still near its bottom, plugged from the inside by a wad of rags on a long oak stick.

Silas took the pot-shaped cap off the still so Tilmon could look inside.

"Scrubbed it over and over, rinsed it good. New clean rags on the plug stick."

"Good. Fill it half full of that there mash but strain it good first."

Silas went back to the shack and began filling smaller buckets from the barrels, pouring the mash through a cheesecloth to catch any floating pieces of ground corn, while Tilmon stacked dried locust wood in the firebox. Chestnut and locust made hot, clean fires and gave off less smoke, so as to minimize any potential clues to their location for a nosy neighbor or a revenue man. It took years of practice to know just how to get the fire just hot enough, but not too hot. The heat from the firebox swirled around the base of the still sitting behind the flames, then vented out the flu in the very back of the groundhog. The temperature had to be just right. A fire too hot caused the mash beer to boil violently and puke up into the cap and the pipes, contaminating the moonshine; not hot enough and the alcohol wouldn't boil off and vaporize.

With the sun high, they sat down to eat from the lunch pail and waited for the cauldron to steam. Silas watched Tilmon eat with one hand.

"Who made that for ya?" Silas motioned to the leather sash that Tilmon wore across his chest over his right shoulder. It had a blunt metal hook affixed to it near his left hip.

"My oldest brother made the first one. I can carry things or pull with it sometimes."

"And like when we were plowing, and you tied the reins to it," Silas said.

'Yeah, that's right."

"Mr. Justice, tell me again. What happened to yer hand?"

Tilmon shrugged. "Don't know. Born without it." He began to mix some oat flour and water in a bucket he held between his feet, making the thick paste that they would use to seal the seams and joints on the still when they finished putting it together.

"Does it hurt?"

"No. Ain't there to hurt, is it?"

Silas seemed to contemplate this as he sat silently for a few moments, then replied. "Back in Rabun, we had a three-legged dog once. I guess a bear got to him or something. He did all right."

Tilmon nodded, unsure of how to respond to the dull boy's comment. During a lifetime without a hand, he'd fixed up plenty of workarounds and figured out how to get along. Some things were always more difficult, but he thought he did all right, too.

"What things are hard for you? With only one hand, I mean."

Tilmon answered quickly. "Can't play the fiddle," he said, glancing sideways at the boy.

Silas seemed taken aback but then smiled uncomfortably, perhaps unsure if this was meant as a joke.

Tilmon laughed to relieve the tension. Then he added, "Buttons on pants is tough. When I was a kid, my momma fixed me up some pants made special. Had bigger pockets and 'spenders. Had a flap on the front that hooked the left, so I could hold 'em up with this here elbow and work the button with my right hand." They sat in silence for a few minutes, then Tilmon continued. "Gotta do things in a certain order, or ya can't do 'em. Like cutting something or pouring—cause you can't hold nothin' with a hand that's missin'— but you learn that after a time or two."

Silas stared into the flames at the mouth of the firebox as though he was trying to imagine how that would work.

"Hardest thing ever' day is tyin' knots, but I can use this here sash hook to help with that sometimes." He thought a minute more. "An' pro'lly shootin'—that's hard. Prop the gun up like this." Tilmon raised his left arm and hung his right hand in the fleshy knob at his elbow. "I'n get to th' trigger with th' butt down here but can't sight too good." He gestured with his left shoulder pulled far forward to raise the elbow in front of him and his right shoulder back and down. This forced his head down as he looked awkwardly along an imaginary barrel. "Never been a good shot. Don't really matter, though. Ain't got no gun."

The steam began to rise from the open top of the still.

"Here she goes," said Tilmon. "Let's put the cap on and get that likker."

Silas retrieved the copper pot that had a pipe sticking out of the side and set it upside-down in the mouth of the still.

"Put that big rock on top to hold her down," said Tilmon, "then seal up the seams." He handed Silas the paste.

The arm pipe connected to a pipe running down into a barrel that had six inches of weak moonshine standing in the bottom—leftovers from a prior run. The vapor from the boiling corn-mash beer eventually percolated up through those backins with a thumping, bubbling sound and pressurized the barrel. This forced the fortified hot vapor out through another pipe, spiraling, worm-like, down around the inside of a second barrel, that was cooled by a constant stream of water they piped over from the branch. The alcohol vapor condensed in the worm-pipe, and the liquid trickled out from the end that poked out of the bottom of the cooling barrel.

About an hour later, the thump keg started percolating; then Tilmon watched for the run to appear. It began to gurgle and spurt. From his pocket, Tilmon pulled a white stick about five inches long. It was bowed slightly in the middle with a short, sharp bend near the end. He stuck it into the worm, and the liquor followed the curve down to the hooked end of the stick and trickled into the collecting jar as a smooth thin stream.

"What's that?" asked Silas.

"Racoon's pecker bone."

He looked at Tilmon uncertainly.

"You know," said Tilmon, grabbing his crotch, "from his pecker."

Silas chuckled slightly. "Oh."

After Tilmon threw out the first contaminated bit, he collected the thin stream of clear moonshine in bottles and jars, filtering it first through a cloth-lined funnel full of coals. They sat and watched and monitored and collected for the next several hours. When he'd filled the tenth jar, he sealed it tightly and shook it, then held it up to watch the bubbles.

"Whatcha doin'?" asked Silas.

"Run is getting weaker, 'bout ready to break." Tilmon pointed at the worm. "Stream is getting' thinner there. Them bubbles is smaller and take longer to break up." He stuck his finger under the stream of moonshine and tasted it, shaking his head. He could tell the potency was way down. "All the rest can be backins for the next run. Set all that aside, an' then we'll break 'er down, an' you can clean it tonight. We'll go again tomorrow."

"How many more times?" asked Silas.

"Till all the mash in them barrels is gone. Pro'lly four or five more days. If we'n get ten quarts per run that'll be good." Tilmon put one jar under his arm and supported it with another one held in his hand as he headed to the shack. The contents were too precious to try to carry more and risk dropping one. Silas followed with a jar in each hand, and they stored them carefully in crates under the cot in the shed.

"I'm hungry."

"Me too. Annie'll have us some cornbread and beans later tonight, but you'll have to come back an' stay here to clean an' keep watch. Keep them sneakers and lookers away."

Just the presence of someone in the still house was enough to deter most, but Tilmon didn't know what Silas would do if someone did show up to raid the place. They had no gun, no bell. No way to notify someone if there was a problem.

Across the valley, near the top of River Mountain and about a half mile up from Tilmon's cabin, Old Man Godard sat in a rocker on his front porch and looked out over the hills toward the sunset. He noticed the shimmering heat rising from a green patch of laurel nestled down in a cleft, and he cussed under his breath.

"Damned moonshiners."

Chapter Four

Sunday, December 5, 1886

From up on the distant hill, a man and a woman came down the trail toward the branch. Bundled in her coat with a scarf around her red hair, Eveline Godard was younger and more sprightly, sure-footedly negotiating the path that she traveled to the Settlement several times each week. Every so often, she stopped to wait on her husband, a much older man who was slightly stooped with a long snow-white beard that made him look even older than the old he was. He jabbed his cane at the ground, then took two steps, repeating the maneuver over and over again, as he slowly made his descent, with his puffs of breath visible in the chilly morning air like smoke from an old narrow-gauge locomotive.

"Might shoulda left earlier. I want a good seat at church," said Eveline, reaching up to give the old man a hand. He waved her away with a scowl and a shake of his head, turning sideways to step down from a rock on the path.

Their destination was the Smyrna church, a little wooden structure that couldn't seat more than thirty people in its bare and unheated single room. No bell called the Settlement to worship— folks just seemed to know when it was about time and made their way down from their cabins to meet on the Sabbath. On this day of rest, there was no hurry to start or stop the service, so they commenced when the preacher was ready and when everyone was gathered. Most everyone, anyway. Eveline came every week, but her husband never did.

Today, when he entered the church behind his wife, the old man silently surveyed the congregation as he made his way down the side aisle, stopping to take a seat by the window. Everyone turned to see, some with faint smirks and nods.

"Look who's here," someone whispered audibly.

Next year he would be seventy—the oldest man in the Settlement by a good ten years. He was wiry, short, and short-tempered. Some of the kids called him "The Sheep" because of his white hair and long white beard, but to most folks, he was just "Old Man Godard."

As Eveline took a seat beside him, he met the eyes of the preacher, Reverend Elisha Eller, who didn't smile, but nodded approvingly as he approached the pulpit to start the service.

"Glad to see y'all today. Beautiful mornin'. 'Specially happy we got our *whole* community gathered here today. Welcome, Mr. James Godard." The short minister was a dour and pious man. He was serious about the salvation of his flock, committed to his ministerial duties, and rarely jovial. He wore a dark suit of clothes and a tie that was bowed at the neck above two very long tails.

There was a faint murmur in the congregation, but Godard gave no reply, made no acknowledgment.

The preacher led the group in a song they all knew, then opened his worn Bible to read a passage from the Book of Revelation.

Throughout the service, when Godard wasn't paying attention, or if he made noise by moving his feet around to keep them warm, Eveline pushed her elbow into his ribs, admonishing him as though he was a little child instead of being the oldest, and practically the only literate person in the room. This latter point added irritation to the already maddening fact that he'd been coerced to be there this day, sitting on the cold, hard bench. He pulled his coat tightly around him and rubbed his arms.

Just leave me in peace to sleep, so long as I don't snore. Bad enough to have to be here, he thought. He was mad at himself for giving in to Eveline and to the preacher, who had finally badgered him enough to extract the promise of attendance this week. At the time, it seemed like a reasonable concession to get the long-winded man to leave their home, but he was still angry at her for inviting the preacher up to their cabin for the visit in the first place. She knew how he felt about church. Later, when he'd attempted to back out of the commitment, she gave him an uncharacteristically stern rebuke and swore she'd never cook him another meal if he didn't go.

"Need to git right with God," she nagged. "Won't live forever, y'know. What'll you say for yerself when you meet up with God?"

"According to their deeds, accordingly, he will repay fury to his adversaries!" Reverend Eller carried on with increasing fervor and not even a hint of stopping soon.

Godard's mind drifted back to memories of a childhood filled with many long and fiery sermons at the dinner table in Pike County, down below Atlanta. His father had been a Primitive Baptist preacher, too—somber and judgmental at home, making an onerous existence for the youngest son who wanted more fun out of life. He remembered that girl Tamsy. She'd been the first of a few. They'd met through members of the church conference, and she immediately caught his eye. Tamsy was a tiny pixie of a lass, with her long hair braided and pinned on top of her head. She was vivacious and engaging. He saw their marriage as a way to escape his father, but both of them were too young: eighteen and sixteen. She'd had a baby just over a year later—then two more. It was after the children came that she changed. She wasn't fun anymore; she became too smothering, too serious, and too stern. It was the corn that had lured young man Godard away in pursuit of fun. Away from his family.

His eyelids drooped...

* * *

Staggering home again, his head swam, and he bent over to throw up in the ditch. Strangely, that made him feel better in a few minutes, and he got a second wind to make it the last quarter mile home. At the door, the string that lifted the latch on the inside had been pulled back through the hole. He rattled the handle furiously, yelling for his wife and kids.

"Tamsy! Lemme in! Where's them kids? William! Joseph! Anna!

He shook the door again, then backed up a step and kicked at the handle, breaking the latch with the second blow. The door flew open violently.

"James Godard, you get out!" she screamed from behind the kitchen table. "You're drunk and disgraceful—shouldn'a never married you!" The swelling from last week's row was going down, but the bruise under her eye was still purple and ugly. Trembling and wild-eyed, she waved a knife at him from behind the table. He knew she didn't have the will to use it.

"Where's my kids? I wanna see my boy! William!" He threw a chair aside and grabbed her arm, wrenching the knife from her hand and throwing it across the room. He pushed her down against the wall and leaned over her with a reeling head and unsteady legs.

"Where's he at?" James raised his fist.

He heard the click of the gunlocks as his father-in-law stepped in through the back door.

"Get out. Now." Will Buckalew raised the double-barrel gun and pointed it at James' head. He spoke in a calm, firm tone. Tamsy scrambled away and stood behind her father.

"Where's William and Joseph? Where's the baby?"

"Get out," Buckalew said again, louder this time. "Don't come back here ever again."

"It's my house, old man." Somewhere from the direction of the hen house outside, he heard the children crying.

Buckalew raised the barrel slightly and pulled one of the triggers, blasting bird shot into the wall with a deafening noise and filling the room with smoke. "I said, get out. Now!" He took a step forward but remained out of Godard's reach. The barrels of the gun peered into James' face like owl eyes, one of them smoking faintly. "Now. Don't you come back, or I swear—I'll kill you."

James raised his hands and moved slowly as Buckalew backed him out of the house, down the steps, and into the yard.

"I need my things."

"Everything here is for her and the kids."

"I need some money."

"You drank all your money, Godless heathen. Go. NOW!" He stepped down off the porch as James staggered backward. Buckalew followed with the gun leveled directly at him, out of his reach but within certain killing distance, finally stopping at the gate. When James was twenty yards down the road, Tamsy appeared at the cabin door with a baby on her hip and two little ones clutching her skirt. She was crying.

He turned to go.

* * *

Godard's head jerked upright as Eveline pressed her elbow into his ribs again.

The preacher raised his voice, leaned over the pulpit, and tried with all his might to scare his congregation's souls into righteousness. "Hell may be waiting for you, and it has all the patience in the world! It knows that every soul that departs this life without the salvation of God will enter into its mouth and burn forever in its agony!" He pounded his fist on the podium as the congregants nodded and murmured in assent.

Godard turned back to his own thoughts, staring through the clear pane window and reflecting on his life. Long decades of bad decisions, fueled by selfishness and lust and the corn, had created a trail of conflict that left him embittered and semi-reclusive in the mountain wilderness; a failure at his career, at odds with his neighbors, estranged from his siblings, and divorced from the wife that bore his only children—but he couldn't see any of it as faults of his own. Over the years, he'd wondered what happened to those three kids: in no way remorseful or emotional, but just as a matter of fact. Maybe he should have gone looking for them when he got assigned to duty down at the hospital in Augusta during the war, but it was too late to worry about that now. That was over twenty-five years ago. *"Can't do what you didn't. Can't un-do what you did."*

Long past noon, when the congregation was clearly getting restless, the preacher finally quit. He had them stand and sing every verse of "Be Ready All" to put a final exclamation point on the sermon and to remind them of *"the awful day that's coming, when heaven's trump shall sound."* Then, after a lengthy and pointed benediction reiterating their looming mortality, the service was finally over.

Godard stretched to relieve the pain inflicted by the hard bench, then he and Eveline worked their way outside with the others. As he'd anticipated, Charlie Rogers was the first come to greet them. He was younger than Godard, and the bit of extra weight he carried gave him a slightly less anemic, less tired appearance than everyone else. He was the only one at church today who wore a matching jacket and pants.

He smiled broadly as he approached, practically clamoring over the others with his hand outstretched, "Well, if it isn't my neighbor James Godard! Happy to see you joining us here at church today." He grabbed Godard's hand and shook it almost violently, then turned to Eveline and removed his hat. "Good morning, Mrs. Godard. How are you?"

"Good morning, Colonel," she said. "We are fine. Not too cold today, thankfully. How's Caroline and the family?"

"Everybody's good, thank you much," replied Rogers. He turned back to Godard. "James, I hope you're gonna start comin' to church meeting every week."

Godard bristled at being addressed by his first name but didn't comment on it. He harrumphed slightly. "Wouldn't count on it."

Among all the people in the Settlement, none of whom had much, Rogers seemed to have enough. Though never dressed in new, he and his wife Caroline always looked the nicest. Godard thought he was hokey, that he walked around like he owned the place, and it galled him. As the unelected leader of the community, Rogers was so esteemed that the creek bore his name. He doled out advice and was called upon by others to arbitrate disputes and settle business. Godard resented it, thinking Rogers always seemed to make too much of a show. He felt that the leadership role should have been his own, since he had actually been trained in the law and was, in fact, the oldest member of the community—at sixty-one, Rogers was eight years his junior. Almost as if to add further insult, Rogers allowed the honorific appellation of 'Colonel' to float around, despite the fact that he hadn't even been in the war. He'd only been in the home guard, and Godard knew that he couldn't even read.

"Two weeks and some days till Christmas. Sure you oughta come then?" said Rogers.

"Might not be here. Got invitations to visit in Atlanta."

"But we'll surely be at church if we're here," said Eveline, pulling James away before he could embellish the lie. "So nice to see you, Mr. Rogers. We need to get on, but do tell Caroline hello for me and let her know that I'll stop by in a few days."

Godard rolled his eyes at Eveline's fawning. *Don't be so dang nice; you'll just encourage him. God forbid his wife shows up at our house.* He turned to follow her without a goodbye.

The couple headed up the path toward River Mountain, below which, on the farther north side, they had a cabin and a few acres of land cleared, but before leaving sight of the church, they stopped again to speak to another group that included several of their nearest neighbors. The ladies exchanged pleasantries and talked about nothing while the children ran about. Godard couldn't hide his impatience with the ritual as he greeted few and said little.

Tilmon Justice approached the gathering with his family in tow. At age thirty, he was less than half Godard's age, but he was weathered from working outdoors. While he was strong and muscular, he was asymmetric. His left sleeve was cut short and tied around the calloused and withered nub that hung below his elbow. The missing forearm was a marked deficiency in an otherwise perfectly normal family man and farmer. In his right hand—his only hand—he carried the family's Bible, which he tucked under his left arm so that he could remove his hat to greet the couple. His wife, Annie, who was clearly pregnant, held the hand of a young boy and struggled to keep a smaller girl on her hip. The Justices were Godard's nearest neighbors; their property lay on the down side of his to the southeast. Godard felt his jaw tighten as the young man approached.

"Mr. Godard," said Tilmon. "Can I have a word," he asked, motioning him away from the group.

Godard followed him a few steps toward the branch, where they stood in a small clearing under the leafless hardwoods. "You need something?" He crossed his arms and looked at the younger man with a cool detachment.

"Been out hunting this week. Seen you been walkin' in my field up there below the path to yer place."

"My field, you mean. Path runs through my field."

Justice's voice hardened. "Path is the line. The part on my side of the path is my field."

"I told you before; the line is down at the Spanish Oak tree. Everything above that is mine," said Godard.

Justice's face flashed red. "Listen here, old man, you saw me puttin' my wheat down in th' upper field last month, and you didn't say nothin', 'cause you know it's my place."

Godard scoffed. "What I saw was you tresspassin', and what grows on my land is mine, as far as the law says."

"Rogers sold me that parcel when we married. I got the deed filed at the courthouse, and you know it. You mess with my crop, you gonna be sorry."

"What do you know about a deed?" Godard glared at the younger man contemptuously. "Carryin' that Bible around is a laugh, to be sure—you can't even read. I'm an attorney; I know my rights, and I know the law. I should report you for hunting on my place." He leaned forward and added smugly, in a low tone, "You better mind your own damned business, or I'll tell some folks I know about *your* business."

Justice's eyes widened and he sputtered with rage, raising both his voice and his clenched fist. "I swear, old man, I'll kill you if you do!" Several people turned to see the disturbance as Justice wheeled around and stomped off. He nearly ran over Jonathan Nicholson, the shoemaker, who had his wife Elizabeth on his arm.

"Tilmon," Nicholson raised his hat and said loudly. "How's them new boots workin' out for ya?"

Justice scowled, not returning the greeting. "They fit fine enough to stomp ol' Godard into the mud. Dang ratbag." He passed his wife, Annie. "Let's go," he barked. She hurried to catch up as he marched up the hill toward home, calling for their son Isaac to follow.

Chapter Five

SUNDAY, DECEMBER 5, 1886

When Godard rejoined the group in the clearing, the others appeared uncomfortable. No one commented about the scene they'd all just witnessed.

Eveline helped make the couple's departure with a few niceties, but as she and Godard started up the same path, she inquired quietly. "James, what in the world?"

"He keeps tryin' to cheat on the boundary," he blurted, loud enough for the others to hear. "Can't face up to the fact that the line between our place and his is down at the oak. Says so right there in the county deed book!"

"Well, maybe you an' him ought to go see Charlie Rogers and come to an agreement."

Godard was instantly infuriated. Eveline recoiled and took two quick steps up the hill to stay out of reach as he stopped abruptly and waved his cane in the air.

"I'll do no such a damned thing! Don't ever call that man's name out to me again! First of all, if anyone should be making decisions up here in this crap hole, it's me, not that uppity windbag. Second, Tilmon's wife is kin to Rogers' wife, so there's no way I'd get a fair deal. And another thing!" Godard screamed. "I don't aim to go an' sit through another one of Eller's long-winded, terrible sermons again for as long as I live! You hear me?"

"Well, all right then, don't work yerself into an apoplexy 'bout it. Just an idea."

"Terrible idea," he said bitterly.

The couple made their way toward home, walking in silence through the bare winter trees. A few of the hills had two routes to the top; one running sideways upward at a gentler angle, back and forth before reaching the top; and another running straight up, the route usually taken by animals or younger travelers. Eveline mostly took the straight-up paths, but she always waited for him at the top. Just before they got to their property, they stopped at the last hilltop to look northwest through a break in the trees. A wisp of smoke hung over a grove of laurels at the base of a ravine on the far side of the adjacent hill. The border with North Carolina lay far out in the hazy distance beyond.

"Down there in that grove," muttered Godard. "Lookee there, got that set up in there. He's too dumb to even hide it good—easy place to find if you're lookin'. Damned moonshiners."

"Don't go getting all riled up about it," said Eveline. "You're not involved. Not your land. No reason for you to pay one bit of attention. Remember what happened—"

"I remember!" he snapped. "Got cheated, got beat, got my barn burned, an' got run out of town. Thought I left that mess down there in Hiawassee, but now it's followin' me."

"All that happened 'cause you were in on it, and you're lucky you didn't get worse. Don't get involved. Mind your own business."

Godard harrumphed and started down the backside of the hill ahead of his wife. Twenty steps later, a young man rounded a corner and met them on his way uphill, his arms full of thick hardwood branches and sticks.

"G'mornin' sir, ma'am," he said when he saw the couple. He dropped the load of wood as he took a big step off the trail to make room for them to pass and snatched his hat from his head before casting his eyes downward.

Eveline stopped to speak to the boy, but Godard stomped by without acknowledgment and continued on with his rhythm of stick-poking and two-stepping. At the bottom, he crossed the field, passed the Spanish Oak, and continued up through the cleared area toward his house. In the distance, he could see the back side of their neighbor's cabin. Godard left the path and marched through the newly sown field in spite, dragging his feet on purpose as he headed back up the last rise toward their home. As he crested the hill, he came to the back of his woodshed and stopped, slightly breathless. It was just a hundred yards more to the porch, but it wasn't the burning in his lungs; it was the ache in his legs from the uphill walk that forced him to rest. He switched hands with his cane and reached out to lean against the wall briefly. A gentle breeze in his face brought the smell first—not a bad smell, but a definite presence. The beast sniffed and snorted. Godard froze and held his breath. The next few seconds seemed to last forever while the animal continued to forage around the corner, only a few feet away, just out of sight, and unaware that the human had returned. Godard stepped back silently, but he lost the grip on his cane, and it clattered against the wall as it fell to the ground. It was then that the beast appeared from behind the far side of the shed. Two steps more, and it came into full view. Deep brown eyes framed the tan muzzle and a drooling maw. A shiny black coat draped over a pair of powerful shoulders. Two-inch claws curled out from the ends of thick, padded fingers. It bellowed and stood on its hind legs, towering over Godard, who stumbled sideways and fell to his knees. He raised one arm momentarily in defense but then covered his face with his hands. He couldn't look. *Please don't kill me.* Godard waited. He held his breath, anticipating a painful, fatal blow.

But nothing happened. The bear snorted. Leaves rustled. When Godard finally dropped his hands and opened his eyes, it was gone. He exhaled and collapsed onto the dirt, his heart racing. After a few minutes, he struggled to his feet, recovered his cane, and made it the last hundred yards through the gate and to the porch, where he sat and tried to calm himself.

He thought about some of the more violent events of his recent past and the liquor that had fueled them. Up here in the mountains at Charlie's Creek, the Smyrna congregation wasn't quite as bad as other church folk Godard had known. Not so hypocritical with regard to the corn. The ones at the Fodder Creek Primitive Baptist Church, back when they'd lived down in town—that lot expected him to pass the liquor out the back door on credit and then to have him fix things for them in court for free, too. But there they all were, at the church every Sunday in their dark suits, lined up like crows. They ran the signals and the money and the jars through his law office, making him part of their schemes; initially only guilty in the spirit of the law, but later in the fullness of its letters, then not even paying him the agreed-upon share. Godard had become so fully entangled in their messes that he took the fines for tippling on Sunday; forty dollars apiece—on seven occasions! That other little incident with McConnell and the knife should have been kept quiet, but McConnell's wife called the sheriff over just a few little cuts on her husband's arm. Godard got thrashed in retribution the next day, so Judge Wellborn threw the whole thing out, calling it even. Still, the town talked about it for months on end.

His reputation suffered, what with the fines and the fighting and the gossip, and he couldn't attract nicer clients. Eventually, the law practice failed. When he was down to his last dollar, and the moonshiners wouldn't pay up, then it was easy enough to take the reward money from the revenuer for naming names. The murder of crows came to exact their revenge in the night, beating him badly and burning down his barn. It was then that Eveline made him sell their place in town and move to the Settlement in the mountains. That had been five years ago, but the stench of his unsavory past seemed to cling to him wherever he went.

In a few minutes, Eveline appeared on the same trail coming up the hill from behind the shed.

He scowled. "Who was that back there?"

"Young man named Silas. Said he's over here from Rabun for work." She came through the gate and secured it behind her.

"Stealin' my firewood?" he asked, working his way out of the chair with his cane for support.

"Not everything out there on that hill is yours, you know. Said he was stayin' with Annie and Tilmon Justice. I guess he's gonna help in their fields through the summer.

"More likely workin' at that dang still."

"He was sweet. Simple, but sweet." She pushed open the door to the cabin and backed up, allowing him to enter first. "What happened to you?" she asked, looking him up and down.

Godard looked down at the dirt on the front of his coat and brushed it off angrily. "I fell." He marched in and sat by the stove with his coat still on, opened the fire door, and added some small sticks to the embers.

"You know, I am gonna go say something to Charlie Rogers. That Justice is breakin' the law and leading that young man astray," he fumed. "And sowing in my field to boot," he barked. "I shouldn't mind that as much. I might get some wheat bread out of it this spring." He gave Eveline a withering look. "Can't you make nothing but cornbread?" he said irritably.

"If all you got is corn, then all you get is cornbread—if you're nice and say 'please' once in a while, that is," said Eveline.

* * *

Three days later, Godard awoke in a particularly unpleasant mood. He'd dreamed about the encounter with the bear and about getting run out of town in Hiawassee. His resentment of the hypocrisy of the churchgoing townspeople burned like bile in his throat.

Eveline was still in the bed beside him, breathing deeply and regularly as she slept.

"Gimme some breakfast," he said as soon as he woke up. "I want grits and bacon." He elbowed her in the back.

Eveline gave no reply but just rolled over and sighed before she worked her way to sitting. "We got that, but we're gonna need some more salt and some other things." She rubbed her eyes. "I'll need to go down to Galloway's later. Maybe there will be some flour."

Godard looked out the window. The skies were clear, and there didn't appear to be any wind. "My knee don't hurt, so not likely to rain today," he said. "I'll go with you."

"I can go by myself; I'll be all right," said Eveline, perhaps a bit too eagerly.

Godard glared at her. "I'll go if I damned well want to, and I said I want to, so I'm going."

Eveline sighed and got up to fuel the stove and start the water for grits.

Later, on their way to Galloway's, they met Charlie and Caroline Rogers, headed back from the store to the Settlement.

"Good morning, James. Eveline." Rogers removed his hat and nodded to her. Caroline and Eveline smiled at each other in greeting. "Headed to trade?" he asked.

"Gettin' supplies, same as you," said Godard flatly.

"Did they have any white flour?" asked Eveline, hopefully.

"No," said Caroline. "No such luck. I 'spect it'll be spring before we see any up here."

"Oh, pity," said Eveline.

"Well, it's something to look forward to," said Caroline, smiling. Godard wrinkled his lip sightly at her simpering and optimism.

"Good to see you at church last Sunday. I hope we will again," said Rogers.

"Definitely not," said Godard. "I'm not sitting on that hard bench for that long ever again."

"Well, you could bring a pillow to sit on, couldn't you?" offered Caroline sweetly.

Eveline put her hand on Godard's arm and intervened as he opened his mouth to reply. "That is such a wonderful idea. I've got some leftover cloth at home. Maybe I'll work on that."

"Will you be home on Christmas eve? The Parker boys are going to take the little ones out for serenading that night. I could make sure they come to see y'all for a song," said Caroline.

"Trespassing on private property, disturbing the peace, and making mischief?"

Rogers chuckled. "Just a little fun for the kids."

"We might be home, but having kids out at night makin' noise and playin' pranks on old people don't sound like fun. You tell them to keep away from my place," said Godard with a scowl. "And speaking of trespassing, I want you to let Tilmon Justice know to stay offa my property, too."

"What's the problem?" asked Rogers.

"He's up on my land clearing and planting. He knows good and well that the path to my place is on my land, and the line between us is at the Spanish Oak. I'll harvest anything that grows on my land; I will."

"James, I don't really remember exactly how it's all laid out. I'll have to walk by down there and see."

"You do that, and you tell him to keep off. And another thing! Did you know he's runnin' a still over near Wheeler Knob there by the branch?"

39

"Well, I know there's lots of folks makin' a little bit of moonshine. Just a hobby. For personal and medicinal use only, I'm sure."

"Nobody makes whiskey just for themselves. Selling is illegal."

"Now, James, I've known you take a sip once in a while—"

Godard cut him off and raised a scolding finger. "I am a man of the law! Anything I ever had was fully legal. What's more, Eveline said he's got himself a young man out there workin' at it with him." He became more agitated and raised his voice further. "Corrupting the youth—that's what he's doin'! Makin' illegal liquor and corrupting youth! This ought to be reported to the authorities. I have half a mind to tell the revenuer I know down in town. When he's in jail, that'll keep him off my land!"

Eveline spoke up. "We really need to be gettin' on. Mr. Rogers, it was so nice to see you again." She took her husband by the arm, urging him to make their departure. "So nice to see you, Caroline."

"Please stop in to visit when you come by," said Caroline.

"I certainly will," said Eveline as she tugged at her husband's arm, finally overcoming his inertia and mulishness to get him moving down the path.

Charlie Rogers shook his head and donned his hat, and the couple headed towards home.

Chapter Six

Friday, December 24, 1886

"Charlie, someone's on the front porch. Get the door, will you?" Caroline Rogers put down the spoon and covered the pot on the stove, wiping her hands on her apron. "An' we're gon' need more firewood," she called out to no one in particular. Nobody budged.

The Rogers' daughter Lucinda, and her husband, Osborne Seay, were sitting at the kitchen table while he was putting the finishing touches on a toy gun whittled from a stick: a Christmas present for one of the kids.

"Os, did you hear me? We need some more firewood."

"Yes'm," said Osborne. He was nearly forty, and he and Lucinda lived over the hill further north with their children, where, like everyone else, they farmed to raise what they needed.

"And Lucy, I could use some help getting things on the table," she added.

Charlie Rogers opened the door to a cold wind that whipped the flames of the candles standing on the window ledges, making them dance and wave.

"Annie, Tilmon! Welcome!" said Rogers when he saw the Justice family on the front porch. "So glad to see you here. Come on in."

Annie tucked a basket under her arm and gave her uncle a hug. The family followed her in.

"Isaac is excited to go serenading tonight," said Tilmon. He put down two-year-old Lura to shake Rogers' hand, and their older son, Isaac, ran over to the corner to see the Christmas tree. They'd cut down the good-sized pine yesterday—tried to, at least. The saw got bound up in the trunk as the tree leaned, and Rogers had to finally shoot the trunk with a couple of blasts from the shotgun to free the saw from the pinch. When it was down, he gave the bottom of the trunk a clean cut, and they dragged it home, where Caroline and Lucinda decorated it with tiny, whittled toys, paper cut-outs, and strings of popcorn. Store-bought candies were tied to some of the branches, but the lowest limbs had already been picked clean, and Isaac couldn't reach the ones up higher. He pointed to one of the top branches and called for his mother, who came over and retrieved the prize for him. Lura toddled away in the opposite direction, too close to the double shotgun standing in the corner for Tilmon's liking. He picked up the weapon and hung it back on the rack over the fireplace mantle.

"It'll be a big old time, for sure," said Rogers. "I told them not to stay out too late."

"He's just five, Tilmon, really," said Annie, apparently revisiting the subject with her husband, as she gave him a concerned look. "What if he gets separated from the group?" She turned to her Uncle Charlie. "Don't you think that's too young to be out at night?" she asked. "He's too young, you don't think?" She searched for an ally to keep Isaac in, but her uncle shook his head and chuckled.

"Naw, they'll be fine. The older ones will watch out for 'em," Rogers said. "Gotta let 'em grow up a little at a time. I told the Parker boys to have everybody back here by midnight. They'll keep track of everybody." Rogers finally took notice of the lanky teenager standing silently behind Tilmon. "Who's this here? This your new helper?" He stuck out his hand to greet the newcomer. "Charlie Rogers. Welcome, welcome. I been wantin' to meet you."

The boy took off his hat, and they shook. He swallowed, looked briefly at Mr. Rogers, then at Tilmon before he just smiled sheepishly and stared at the floor in silence.

"This is Silas," said Tilmon. "I know his daddy from over in Rabun, and Silas here is helpin' me 'round the place. Been here a few weeks now.

"Well, Silas, that's just fine. What's he got you working at?"

Silas appeared to contemplate this question. He opened his mouth slightly a couple of times as if to speak, but no words came. As the pause became uncomfortable, he looked at Tilmon, who answered for him.

"We been clearing more in the upper field for planting," he said.

"That sounds good. Winter wheat?" asked Rogers.

"Yeah, if we can keep the birds off it," said Tilmon. "And the neighbor,' he added sourly. Silas still said nothing, but glanced at Tilmon, then at Mr. Rogers, and smiled weakly. Rogers looked back and forth between the two, then let it drop.

The house buzzed with excitement as more of the locals gathered for the festivities. On Christmas Eve each year, the Rogers' home was the hub for a family and community party in the late afternoon as the sun set. Their place was the largest in the Settlement. It started out as a two-room cabin, pretty much the same as the others, but over the years, they'd added onto it as their family grew. The original construction was the center of the home, with the seating areas and a kitchen. It had a table, a pot belly stove, a larder, and the door to the porch on the back of the house. Each of the new additions had two small bedrooms with fireplaces. The expanded size of the Rogers' home relative to the others in the area, and Rogers' leadership in the Settlement made it the natural focus of community and social life.

Annie set her basket on the table and took off her coat.

"Somethin' smells good,' said Rogers, lifting a corner of the cloth tucked into the top of the basket and leaning over it to take in the aroma. "What ya got?"

"Apple stack cake," said Annie. "Grandmama's recipe." Annie pulled off the cover to reveal a stack of six very large, very thick pancakes, alternating with layers of chopped and mashed apples in a sweet brown syrup.

"Mmm, my favorite," he replied.

"Honey, that looks beautiful," said Caroline coming over from the stove. "Where'd you get the flour? I can't hardly find none to buy."

"Oh, I been hidin' it away for months," said Annie.

"An' we ain't had no biscuits at our place since the spring," added Tilmon, his matter-of-factness possibly hiding some irritation. "If my wheat makes, we might have some flour in a few months."

"Well, bring it on down when you get it in, an' I'll grind it for you," replied Rogers.

Sharp steps rang on the front porch before two more teenagers suddenly burst through the front door without knocking.

"Mr. Rogers, I got some more caps for the shotgun. Can we take it out tonight for the serenading?" asked the slightly taller boy, breathless from running up the hill.

"Well, hello, D. L., Merry Christmas to you, too," said Rogers, with a side glance at the youngsters.

"Oh, yes sir, sorry. Merry Christmas, Mr. Rogers." The boy looked around at the others. "Merry Christmas, Mr. and Mrs. Justice."

Silas remained silent, still one awkward step away from the group.

Tilmon made the introduction. "This is Silas," he said to the boys.

"Hey, I'm David Parker. Folks call me D. L., and this here is my brother James." He extended his hand.

Perhaps more at ease with the boys nearer to his own age, Silas seemed finally emboldened to speak. "We both have Bible names," he said with a chuckle. He didn't shake hands, but he wiped his chin with the back of his hand and began rocking back and forth slightly, breaking eye contact with Parker and looking alternately at his shoes and over his shoulder to the kitchen. "I know another boy named David, but I never heard of nobody else named Silas, 'cept Silas in the Bible. I was named for Silas in the Bible. I wasn't named after my daddy because his name ain't Silas. His name is Jason. Were you named for David in the Bible?

"I suppose so. Never thought about it, really," said Parker, with a questioning glance at Mr. Rogers, who nodded encouragingly.

"Well, was your daddy named David?"

"No, my daddy's name is Jehu."

"Well, that's a name from the Bible." Silas looked at James Parker. "And James is a name from the Bible, and I've got a Bible name too. I'm named for Silas from the Bible."

"Well, all right then," said D. L., looking for an exit. "Mr. Rogers, about the gun, can we take it tonight?"

"Yes, I suppose you can," said Rogers.

"Tell him I get to shoot the gun, too. Tell him, Mr. Rogers," said James urgently.

"Yes, James, you can shoot, too. Your daddy taught y'all both real good, but mind you, keep an eye out for all the little ones. Stay all together."

"We will," said James.

"What all do you have planned?" asked Annie with a concerned look.

James grinned at the prospect of the fun they were going to have. "Well, we got us some cow bells an' some whistles. We gon' sneak on up to the houses and make a racket and shoot the gun to get the 'tention of 'em in there. Then we'll sing 'em a Christmas song, an' after that, folks'll have us in for some punch and something to eat."

"No pranks, now," admonished Mr. Rogers. "I don't want folks all riled up and comin' to complain about it to me tomorrow."

"No sir. We won't," said James, but the knowing glance he gave his brother didn't instill confidence in the promise.

"Can you be sure to keep a close eye on Isaac?" asked Annie earnestly. "How 'bout you do a couple of houses down here first and before you head out further, then when you get to our house, Isaac can stay, an' y'all can go on after that? He's too little. I'm worried 'bout him bein' out at night. It's cold."

Tilmon shook his head at his wife's continued anxiety over an issue which had already been settled.

Rogers reassured her once more. "I think that's a good compromise. I know the boys will take good care. Don't you worry." He turned back to the Parker boys. "When y'all get up there to take Isaac in, I don't want y'all to go on up to Mr. Godard's. When I saw him last week, he didn't seem like he was in a particularly festive spirit, and it'd pro'lly be best to leave him be."

At the mention of Godard's name, Tilmon clenched his jaw. "Dang troublemaker, he is. Y'all stay away from his place."

"Let's go see what my wife needs of us. She asked for somebody to bring in some more firewood," said Rogers.

Just then, Osborne Seay struggled through the back door with a load of wood on his arms, stacked to his nose. D. L. and Rogers helped unload the split logs from his outstretched arms setting them in the corner and under the bench near the fireplace.

"Thanks, Tilmon," said Osborne. "Y'all doin' all right out at your place?"

"Fine, all right," said Tilmon with an unconvincing scoff. Rogers, Tilmon, and D. L. followed Osborne out the back door, headed to the woodshed.

"What's the problem?" Rogers pressed Tilmon as Osborne loaded D. L.'s arms with more of the split logs. "Is it working out okay with the new boy? He seems likable enough, maybe a bit peculiar, but seems nice. Is he a hard worker?"

"He's all right," said Tilmon. "Does what I ask an' learns fast enough. He helped me clear the upper field for wheat an' worked hard at it. His daddy Jason is gon' come visit by here in a couple of weeks on the way to see a sister over towards Titus. He'll need to stay the night. Would it be OK if he can stay here with you then?" he asked Rogers. "We just don't have the room, really."

"Surely," said Rogers. "Always got room for a little hospitality."

"But I tell you what's trouble; it's that damned Old Man Godard. He says the property line's lower down the rise than you and I agreed on, and he marches up through my planted field, draggin' his feet 'cross the furrows out of spite for it."

"He mentioned that y'all weren't seeing eye to eye on that matter when I saw him a couple of weeks ago on the way to Galloway's," said Rogers. "I can go out there and walk the field with you an' him an' come to an understanding."

Tilmon pulled a flask bottle from his pocket and uncorked it with his teeth. He took a swig, then handed it to Osborne. "Godard is so pigheaded he won't give in to nothin'."

Osborne took a drink and passed the flask to his father-in-law.

"D. L., why don't you carry that on inside," Rogers said. The teen looked a bit discouraged at being dismissed from the grown-up ritual, but he took the load of wood up onto the porch and kicked at the door.

With the boy just out of earshot, Rogers continued. "And what about this?" he asked as he lifted the flask and took a small sip. He grimaced, pursed his lips, then shook his head and exhaled with a whistle as the liquor did its work. He gave the bottle back to Justice.

"That business is workin' just fine. Made a good run the last couple of weeks. The next run should sell for enough for me to clear off the debt. I need to get some more runners to take it off up to Carolina and over to Rabun." Tilmon's face soured even further, and the irritation came to a boil as his words spilled out with volume, intensity, and venom. "But damn that Godard. That ratbag said he gon' tell some folks he knows about my business. He oughta be dead for messin' with somebody's living like he does. I'll make him look straight down a double gun if I catch him snoopin' around. If he goes to huntin' my still, he'll never hunt another, I swear it!"

As someone inside opened the door for D. L., a bit of light and the sounds of the growing crowd in the house tumbled out onto the backyard for a moment.

Chapter Seven

SUNDAY, JANUARY 16, 1887

Jason Coward left his Rabun County home north of Persimmon at about noon. He headed nearly due west, uphill on a path only ever traveled by foot, running around the south side of Chestnut Mountain, then back down to cross the Coleman River. He made the crest of the trail by early afternoon, reaching the spot where, if it was clear and if you knew what you were looking for, you could see Hightower Bald in the distance on the border with North Carolina. Today was not one of those days. Overcast, but not as cold as usual. The warmth was a welcomed change, but it allowed the snow to melt wherever the sun shone and made a muddy mess of the trail. In another hour, he reached the bottom, where he met a trail that followed the Tate Branch on its journey southwest toward the Tallulah. Coward moved more slowly now that he was into his fifth decade. The trip to visit his son would take all afternoon. He was going to get Silas, and then the two of them were going on to see his sister who lived down in Titus on the road to Hiawassee. He figured he'd stay at the house of the man that Silas was working for, Tilmon Justice, but with no notice given on the date and time of his arrival, Jason knew he might have to make do with whatever was available—a space on the floor, or maybe even just a loft in the barn. He had brought a rolled quilt tied to the top of his backpack for just such a possibility.

The leafless trees silently guarded the Tate Branch as he marched downward under the shelter of the hills, but when he turned south at the bottom of the valley where it joined the Tallulah River, Jason faced the cold wind head-on. There, the branches rattled and clapped above him in the broad flat where the waters met in a large open area—less than two feet deep but at least thirty yards across with no bridge. Horses and wagons had no trouble crossing here on the firm bottom of small rocks and gravel, but travelers on foot had to cross on the steppingstones. He stopped to survey the expanse before venturing out carefully across the piles of rocks that had been placed by locals. Halfway across and with no warning, his foot slipped, and he suddenly found himself on all fours in the river. The shock of the ice-cold water took his breath away as it filled his boots, and he cursed as he stood to wade across the rest of the knee-deep river. Coward heaved himself up on the bank and sat on a log to remove and empty his boots. He had some spare pants and socks in his bag, but he'd need to dry the inside of his boots. *Dang it,* he thought. *Gotta make the Settlement before dark.* Stopping to make a fire here meant that he'd lose daylight, but he decided to chance it. With a few dead branches, sap-rich scraps of pine, and a couple of pinecones, he eventually started a blaze by using up all but two of the dozen matches he had. After he dried off as best he could, he wrapped up in the quilt and set his boots beside the fire. He had at least two more hours of walking to go.

When his boots were better but still not completely dry, he continued on the trail downriver. The Tallulah flowed smoothly down the narrow valley like a wide, glassy mirror, except for a few areas where it stepped down over rocky barriers. Small clusters of trout sat motionless near the bottom of the river—all facing upstream to let the water run over and through them as they waited for their next meal to float by.

A mile and a half later, he reached the mouth of Charlie's Creek and looked up the gorge at the westbound trail, where the path disappeared over a steep hill—the first of several that lay ahead of him. As he climbed the trail, the creek lay further and further down the steep bank on his left, and the foliage became thick on the equally steep slope on his right. His pace was now much less brisk, just a few steps at a time before he paused briefly to rest or detoured around muddy areas on the path with the winter sun retreating in the distance. It would be dusk soon. He buttoned his coat against the chill, even as he broke a sweat on the uphill walk. His feet were numb.

Coming around a rocky obstacle at the peak of a hill, he caught sight of another traveler moving in the same direction further down the trail. He hurried to catch up. He might need directions or might not make it to Justice's house before dark.

"Hey there," called Coward from the top of a small rise. The man below stopped and turned to look up. He waited as Coward descended the trail.

"Hey there. Where you headed to?" the man asked as Coward came nearer. Along with his backpack, the man carried a fishing pole and a net in one hand, with five good-sized fish hanging from a stringer in his other.

"River Mountain. Goin' to see my son. He's stayin' over near there with a man named Justice."

"Oh yes. Are you Silas's daddy? I'm Charlie Rogers." He maneuvered the poles and the net, and the two men shook hands.

"Yeah, I'm Jason Coward."

"Tilmon Justice is married to my wife's niece. They live pretty close by us. Tilmon asked me a couple of weeks ago if you could stay at our place whenever you come. We got a little more room."

"Well, that's mighty nice. Just stayin' a night or maybe two. Headed over to my sister' down in Titus."

"Well, all right, then. We'll stop by Tilmon's place before we get to mine. Looks like we're havin' fish for supper." He raised his catch, smiling. Four good-sized brown trout and a small rainbow trout hung from the stringer. "Let's get on before it gets dark. Not too far now."

As they approached Tilmon's cabin, Coward pointed out the dim light far up the neighboring hill. "Is that your place, up there?"

"Naw. That's Old Man Godard. He was a lawyer down in town."

"What's he doin' so far from the courthouse? No lawyerin' to do up here."

"He don't lawyer no more. Moved up here in '82. Got run off from town after he got crosswise with some folks."

"Who?"

"People in the stillin' business."

"Was he stillin'?"

"Well, he was in on it some down there, I suppose. Pro'lly not doin' the stillin', but workin' the business with 'em. Didn't go well. Fighting and such. They burned him out. I guess he got enough money to last him without working anymore. Lives up there with his wife, Eveline. No kids. He is a mean ol' cuss. Told me a couple of weeks ago that he was gonna report on Tilmon's stillin' business, but I don't think he'd do it." Rogers chuckled. "Nobody here to tell, and we all know already."

"Silas is working with Tilmon on stillin'?"

"Can't say for sure, but I figure he is. If he's helpin' out on all the work Tilmon's doin', then that's a part of it. Part of life, ain't it?"

"True enough. It's all right if he is. He's needed somethin' diff'rent. Needed some learnin' from somebody else. Bigger community, more folks to know."

They continued up the path with few words between them and reached Tilmon's cabin just as the sun set. Rogers knocked.

Annie opened the door. "Hey, Uncle Charlie," she said, wiping her hands on her apron. "How are you?"

"Doin' good. Brought us a visitor," he said, nodding to Coward. "And some fish." He sat down on the porch step to pull some of the catch free from the stringer. "This here is Silas's daddy. Met him on the trail up from the river."

Jason pulled his hat from his head. "Jason Coward. Nice to meet you. Thanks for takin' Silas in."

Annie nodded from the top step. "Nice to meet you too. We're glad to have him. He's a big help for Tilmon. He's a very polite boy." Two children appeared behind her in the doorway. "This is Isaac and Lura."

Silas came to the door and jumped off the porch to greet his father. "Hey, Daddy!"

"Hey, son, how ya doin'?" he asked, putting one arm around his son's shoulder.

"Fine, all right. I like bein' here. Miss Annie and Mr. Tilmon are real good to me. I miss Momma an' you, though."

Coward patted Silas on the shoulder, then nodded at Isaac and Lura. "Hey, how are y'all?"

"Fine," said wide-eyed Isaac before disappearing back inside. Lura said nothing and kept her thumb securely in her mouth.

"And another one soon?" Coward said with a nod, acknowledging Annie's condition.

"About a month more, I think," she said.

"Got some names picked out?"

"Sarah, after my mother—if it's a girl. Luther for a boy. Do you have other children?"

"Oh, yeah. Ten of 'em, including a set of twins—Mary and Joseph." Coward laughed. "They's six now and really something else, I tell ya. Got four grandchildren now, too."

"We got lots of names from the Bible," said Silas, rocking back and forth slightly.

"That's nice," said Annie.

"Is Tilmon here?" asked Rogers. He stood and handed over two of the fish.

"No. Still out. Pro'lly won't be back till late."

"I'm going back up there now," said Silas. "You can go up there with me to see him. I know the way real good."

"Up where?" asked Coward.

"Back up to where I work at for Mr. Tilmon."

"No need," said Coward. "I can see him tomorrow." He motioned to Silas. "Son, can I talk to you for a minute?" Silas and his father walked a few feet out into the yard.

"You workin' at a still with Tilmon?"

"Sort of. I clean up and collect firewood and such. I don't make the still run."

"That's OK. You know to just keep that sort of thing quiet, right? You could get in some trouble by talking too much about it. That man Godard that lives up the hill up there," Coward gestured with a nod, "You steer clear of him. I just heard that he might tell on folks that's workin' on a still, and you don't need no part of that trouble. Just keep it quiet, all right?"

"Yes, sir. I will."

Rogers spoke up. "Let's get on and get to supper then. Silas, you tell Tilmon that your daddy is here, and he's stayin' at my place like we talked about. He can come over tonight to visit if he wants."

"I'll do that," said Silas.

"I'll come back in the morning," said Coward as he and Rogers turned to go. "Nice to meet you."

In the rapidly advancing darkness, the men made their way down the path around the bottom of the field toward Roger's home. "Follow behind me. I know this path real good. No worry." Coward fell in behind Rogers.

"Well, Jason, what do you do for work?" asked Rogers over his shoulder.

"Got a small place above Persimmon. Farm some, hunt some. This and that. Not much, really. You?"

"Same sort of things we do here, I 'spect."

"Pro'lly."

"You work the land by yourself?"

"Naw, me and my other boys. I was glad for Silas to come out here and work, though. Thankful for Tilmon takin' him in. His momma's worried shore nuff, but I said he'd be all right, and if it didn't work out, he'd come on back home."

Rogers nodded to himself. "Silas seems to be doin' just fine. Helped Tilmon clear this here field and plant." He motioned to the area above them on the left. "And helpin' him with his other business too." As they continued up along the edge of the field, Coward wondered about the lawyer man.

"That old man Godard—should I be worried 'bout Silas in on that business with Tilmon?"

"I don't think so, but I'd just steer clear of Godard, anyway. He's mighty ornery."

When they got to the top of the hill, Rogers pointed down at the dim light from a cabin less than a quarter mile away. "That's my place. We'll get some of this fish cooked up and get you settled in for the night."

They arrived at Roger's house and came through the rickety gate in the stick-and-wire fence that surrounded the place. Rogers announced his arrival by stomping his boots on the steps to kick off the mud before he threw open the door and hollered.

"Hey there!" They stepped into the main room, warmed by the fire and lit with two kerosene lamps. A short, stout woman came in from the kitchen.

"Caroline, this here is Jason Coward," he said as he handed over the fish. "Here from over in Rabun to see his son Silas. You remember—the boy stayin' with Tilmon and Annie?"

"Oh yes. He's such a nice boy. Came over with them on Christmas Eve," she said warmly. "He didn't say too much, but I think he had a good time over here for the party. Charlie, did he go out serenading with 'em that night?"

"No, I don't think so."

"That mighta been a bit much for him, I think," said Coward. "He's a worried sort, generally. I'm glad that Tilmon's givin' him some work. Pro'lly be good for him."

"I 'spect it will," said Rogers.

"Well, Mr. Coward, welcome. Sit on down there by the fire and get warmed up. I'll get these fish ready for frying, and we'll have supper soon," said Caroline.

Coward took off his boots as they sat, putting them nearer to the fire to dry, along with his wet pair of socks. He extended his feet toward the hearth.

"I got a room in the back for you tonight. There's fireplace in there we'n get going. How long will you stay?" asked Rogers.

"Just tonight, thank you. Tomorrow I'll visit with Tilmon for a bit, then collect Silas and head over to my sister's. Might stay there a couple of days."

"Well, stay with us again when you come back through. We'll be glad to have you."

Chapter Eight

Monday, January 17, 1887

Tilmon awoke as the daylight began to glow in the window. Annie slept with her back to him, sunken down into the corn-shuck mattress, under two quilts, breathing in slow deep rhythm. He shifted to his side and draped his right arm over her belly, moving closer to her warmth and taking in the familiar, comforting smell of her hair. She usually made a long braid and pinned it up during the day. Tilmon liked to watch her take the braid down and brush her hair before bedtime. She made him happy. She didn't complain when they were runnin' short, which was near all the time, and she worked hard. She could make supper out of practically nothing and always took good care of the children. *I'm a lucky man.*

Annie stirred and rolled onto her back.

"When did you come in? I waited up for a while, but it got too late. Did you get your supper? Uncle Charlie gave us two nice trout. I left you a plate out."

"Yeah, it was real good. I got in pretty late. Silas stayed up at the still. I'll take something to eat up to him later and fetch him back here tonight."

"I didn't get to tell you yet. Silas's daddy is here to visit. He stayed at Uncle Charlie's last night. He's gonna come over this morning, and then I think they goin' on to visit kinfolk today."

"Yeah, Silas told me. We finished cookin' up the mash and fillin' the barrels for 'em to sit. It's a couple of weeks till they'll be ready to run, so now's a good enough time for him to be gone for a bit. I'll still have to pay Galloway back for the corn, but I should be able to make some profit from the run this time."

Annie looked at him sweetly. "When you finish this run, and we have a little money, can we go down to town for some things? I need to do some sewing, and I want to get some calico. Lura needs a new dress."

"We can do that. We'll get enough for you a new dress, too." Tilmon smiled and rubbed Annie's belly. "And maybe we're gon' need some things for the baby?"

Annie smiled and kissed him. "That will be nice." After a few still minutes together, they heard the children getting up in the front room. Isaac and Lura came in and climbed onto the bed with them.

"What's for breakfast?" asked Isaac.

"Grits. Same as always. You hungry?" asked Annie.

"I'm always hungry," said Isaac.

The words stung. Tilmon knew it wasn't just an exaggeration and felt bad about it. He often felt hungry too but left the food for the little ones—sometimes taking a drink instead. Tilmon rolled onto his back and looked at the ceiling. Since he started stillin' this past year, he'd been at it more. Annie didn't mind him taking a drink, really— hell, she'd have one, too, on occasion. But in the past few months, he could tell she wasn't happy about it—not that she said anything. It was the look on her face. If folks stopped by and they ended up gettin' lit, she'd take the kids and go do something else for a while. He'd started tucking the bottles away so she wouldn't see. *Need to cut down on that.*

Isaac worked his way down between his parents, and Annie ran her fingers through his hair. "Can you go out with Papa and get some more firewood? I'll get the stove going. Go get your pants and shoes on."

Tilmon groaned as he sat up and turned to put his feet on the floor. When he and Isaac were dressed, they headed outside and walked out to the edge of the yard to relieve themselves. They laughed about pissing together outside and waved their water around in the mud by the fencepost. Isaac puttered around in the shed as Tilmon took inventory of his hidden bottles and nipped at one of them.

"Look up there, Papa," said Isaac, "Turkeys."

In the distance, at the top of the upper field, a cluster of large brown birds bobbed along the furrows, pecking and scratching. Intermittently, they stopped and extended their necks, cautiously surveying the area, right and left, before repeating the maneuvers again. Pecking and scratching, looking for their meal, watching for danger.

Tilmon fumed. "Son, them turkeys is eatin' our biscuits! How bout we eat us a turkey for supper instead?" he said. "Get that firewood in for your mama. I'm gonna get the gun from Mr. Rogers. Hurry before they run off." Tilmon took a swig from his flask.

Isaac nodded eagerly and ran to the woodpile to collect the fuel while Tilmon went to the shed and saddled the mare. Once mounted, he took the less direct path to Rogers, using the downward trail first, then headed north, so as to avoid going up by the field and scaring off the birds.

It was just over a mile and a half going that way, and he made quick time. At the Rogers' gate, he jumped down and threw the reins over the rail, then hustled up to the house. Charlie Rogers sat in a chair on the porch and watched the hurried approach. Tilmon mounted the steps in one leap and went straight into the house without a greeting. In a moment, he appeared back on the porch with the double-barrel shotgun.

Rogers pulled the pipe from his teeth. "Well, good mornin', Tilmon," he said with a slight tone of amusement. "In a hurry?"

"Got turkeys in the wheat field." Justice paused to check the gun and threw the satchel of ammunition over his shoulder.

"Well, let me know if you get you one. Jason Coward is here. Came over from Rabun and stayed here last night. Said he was gonna get Silas to go with him today to see his sister."

Tilmon stopped and tucked the gun under his left arm to free his right hand. "Yeah, Annie told me." He took a swig from his flask.

"I'll send him down to your place in a little bit."

"All right then," said Tilmon, distractedly, as he returned to the mare and remounted for the trip home. This time, he took the more direct route—approaching his fields from the bottom of the hill on Rogers' land.

As he neared the top of the ridge, he dismounted at the edge of the woods and tied the mare to a young pine tree. Stepping quietly through the undergrowth at the top of his field, he looked out to see if the birds were still there and positioned the gun over the stump of his left arm in as good a firing position as he could manage. He crouched, motionless for a few minutes. Nothing moved. Tilmon made a few quiet turkey calls and remained stock still, listening for any sign of the birds. Nothing. He took a swig from the bottle again. At the edge of the open field, he moved around the perimeter to his right with quiet, slow steps. Listening and watching. When he reached the shelter of the Spanish Oak on the southwestern side of the upper field but still hadn't seen the birds, he finally relaxed and stood tall. *Dang it.* Tilmon had been looking forward to having the meat. He took a big draw from the bottle again.

On his way back to collect the mare, Tilmon noticed a beaten-down area in the field. It was a new crossing, perpendicular to the furrows, leading down the hill toward the creek—not an animal track. Deep boot prints compressed the muddy ground, running in both directions up and down the newly beaten path, trampling the new wheat sprouts and tearing through the furrows. The rains of the previous week had run down and created a rut, worsening the damage to the field. At the top of the hill, the new trail disappeared into the woods.

He returned to where the mare stood in the tree line and looked beyond her toward the east side of the upper field. Three, then four more trails became apparent. Tilmon walked over to inspect. This was more than just random steps through the new growth. This was clearly not something made by accident. Ugly gashes marched up and down through his crop, where dragging feet kicked through the furrows. Each wound started in the bottom corner of the field at the trail toward Charlie's creek and trampled the new growth, making its way up the hill toward a single destination at the top—the path leading on toward Godard's place.

Dang Ratbag! Tilmon's ears burned. His scalp tingled with rage. He dropped the gun and gritted his teeth as he clenched his fist and screamed at the sky. "*Aaahrgh!*"

He picked up the gun and unhitched the mare, then made his way home down the west side of the field with no prize for dinner, with fury in his belly and with a pounding headache.

Tilmon staggered a bit as he put the mare in the shed without unsaddling her or removing her bit, then pulled a bottle from the rafters and took two large gulps before sitting down on an upturned bucket. *Damned Godard, messing up my field*! He took another swig.

Isaac called to him from the porch. "Papa, momma says grits is ready."

"I'm coming after I finish here. Y'all go on and eat," he yelled back without looking.

He took another gulp of the moonshine and leaned his head against the wall, anticipating the relief from the corn. In the upper field, the turkeys reappeared and continued their foraging. Tilmon knew he was too far away for a kill, but he stood and picked up the gun, bringing it to a firing position on the stump of his arm. At the same time, he knocked over the bucket. It rolled over with a clatter, and Tilmon stumbled on it.

When he looked up again, the turkeys were gone. Tilmon sat and shook his head with disgust. *No turkey, no biscuits.* A few minutes passed; the warmth crept over him. After the next gulp, Tilmon rubbed his mouth with his sleeve. Warmer still. He set the bottle down between his boots as he rubbed the stub of his left arm and surveyed the limb. The corn always brought out the things that he usually tried to keep hidden. Shame. Embarrassment. Anger. The injustice of the absence of this hand filled his thoughts, and he glared at the calloused knob and clenched his teeth. *How come I ain't got no hand?* He took another swallow. *No arm, no schooling.*

He drank again—now numb to the burning assault on his gullet. His head wagged. He had to pee. Tilmon worked his way to standing and managed to cork the bottle and tuck it under his arm so he could lean the gun against the wall. He unbuttoned his pants, pulled a suspender off his shoulder, and worked it down—but then lost his balance, slipped, and pitched backward into the muck behind the shed, dropping the bottle as he landed. *Dammit!*

Another voice from up at the house called down to him. This time it was Annie.

"Tilmon? Tilmon, are you coming in for breakfast?"

"Yeah, in a minute," he mumbled. He tried to sit up, but he suddenly felt his warm water in his pants.

"And we're all out of cornmeal. Can you go to Galloway's this afternoon and see if he'll give you some on credit?" Annie's skirt swished as she came down from the yard. "Tilmon, did you hear me? I need you to go to Galloway's later and get some more corn meal. I just got two potatoes left, an' we can have them tonight. Are you gonna come in and get your breakf—?"

She stopped short when she rounded the corner and saw him flat on his back.

"What in the world? Tilmon!" There he lay in the muck with his saturated pants askew halfway down his thighs. Annie's surprise rapidly turned from concern to disappointment and then to chastisement, as she finally—after months—said something about his mistress corn.

"Tilmon! This is ridiculous. It's barely breakfast, and you're drunk? Look at you!"

He reached for the wall and tried to sit up, but he knocked over the shotgun. The barrel hit him on the head as it fell.

"Gimme that," She stepped forward and picked up the gun. "Like to kill yourself with this gun, but the liquor will do it eventually if you don't straighten up. This is a disgrace. What if the children saw you like this?"

Before Tilmon could respond, Isaac appeared from behind his mother. He surveyed the situation blankly.

"Get on out of here," barked Tilmon, trying to roll over and cover himself.

Annie took the shotgun, grabbed Isaac's hand, and stormed back into the house with the shotgun. She slammed the door.

Tilmon cursed. *Dammit. No money for food, much less calico.* He pushed himself up onto all fours then worked his way to standing by holding onto the wall before looking down at himself. *Covered in piss and muck and hay.* He pulled up his pants and sat on the overturned bucket then looked up at his field on the slope above. *Crops getting eat up and destroyed.* He was furious. *Ratbag Godard!* After retrieving bottle, he stared at it for a moment before he took another drink. *One armed cripple. Havin' to rely on a dimwit for help.* The shame burned. *Pissed your pants in front of your boy.* The humiliation was complete. *Three kids, two potatoes, no money.* His heart sank. *No hope.* The injustice of it all seemed so overwhelming.

As he took two more gulps, the heat of the corn fueled the embers of decades of frustration, years of unrealized dreams, and visions of unending hardship with more mouths to feed. The embers became flames, then an inferno as hot as a groundhog furnace.

Damned Godard!

He wept.

Chapter Nine

◆━━ ● ━━◆

Monday, January 17, 1887

"Thank you for lettin' me stay; I'd better be getting' on now," said Coward as he rose from the table.

"I sure hope you were warm enough last night," said Caroline Rogers. She picked up his plate and turned toward the kitchen. "There's more oatmeal. Do you want another egg?" she asked over her shoulder.

"Plenty warm and plenty to eat, thank you." Coward sat by the fire and pulled on his boots, now completely dried and warmed through. "I was tired after that walk, an' I slept hard."

"Well, now, you're sure welcome to stay here on your way back. Do you know when that might be?" asked Rogers.

"Won't stay at my sister's for more'n a couple of days, I think. I'll need to be getting back. My other sons there will be keepin' up with the chores, but my wife will want me back at home."

"That's so sweet," said Caroline, smiling as she returned to the table.

At the door, Coward shook hands with Rogers and nodded appreciatively at Caroline. "Thank you kindly."

"You're certainly welcome," said Rogers.

Coward started out toward Justice's house, a mile away. The overcast sky hid the sun, so he couldn't estimate the time of the morning, but he knew there'd be plenty enough daylight to get to his sister's without any problem. It wasn't long before he came out of the trees as he crested a hill, where he could see his destination beyond the fields, painted bright green by the sprouts of winter wheat just a few inches tall. He noticed the mess someone made walking through the field as he made his way around the edge down toward Justice's house in the distance.

When he arrived, he found Tilmon sitting by a fire in the yard.

"Tilmon, how ya doin'?" he said as he walked up. He expected Tilmon to stand to greet him, but instead, his head lolled over his shoulder as he attempted to turn and see who had spoken. Justice was clearly well into a bender.

"Hey there, Jason. How ya doin'? Did you get breakfast?"

"Yeah, had somethin' at Roger's house. Is Silas here?"

"No. He stayed out at the..." Tilmon stopped himself.

"Where? Is he okay?"

"Yeah, he stayed over in another little place I got. Come sit with me for a minute, and then we'll go get him," Tilmon slurred as he waved Coward over.

Both men turned as a man coming up the path from below the horse shed called to them.

"Hey, Tilmon," said Elijah Wheeler. The twenty-year-old was another resident of the Settlement who often came by to have a sip with his neighbors. Elijah was someone that Tilmon counted as a friend, having known him since he was just a ten-year-old boy. They had gone fishing together on occasion and he was good company. A young man, just starting out with his new bride, he was still ambitious and optimistic—not yet disillusioned by his life and by the dim prospects they all shared.

"Hey, Elijah, come on over and sit. This here is Jason Coward, a fella I know from over in Rabun. Sit. Sit. Did you bring any corn likker?" Tilmon waved his bottle loosely in the air.

Wheeler laughed. "Looks like you don't need any more this morning. Hell, Tilmon, it ain't even near dinner time yet. I'll sit a spell with you and have a nip, though." He got the bottle from Tilmon and took a drink, then turned to Coward and extended his hand. "Elijah Wheeler. How ya doin'?"

They shook. "Fine enough. How're you?"

"Good. You Silas's daddy?"

"I am," said Coward, warming himself with his hands outstretched to the flames. "You ain't too cold sittin' out here now?" he said to Tilmon.

"Plenty warm." He motioned for Wheeler to return the bottle.

He passed it back to Tilmon, then continued with Coward. "Well, I can let you know this, then. I came over this mornin' to find him. I loaned him a quarter a month or more ago when we was down at Mr. Galloway's store. I need it back."

"What did he need a quarter for?" asked Coward.

"I was down there for supplies. Tilmon was getting corn and had Silas with him. Must a been right after he came over here to work. He's a nice kid, an' he asked me to borrow some money, so he could get some stuff at the store."

"Candy, I bet."

"Ha! Yeah, he got him all kinds." Wheeler laughed and scratched his head. "I don't know he had any change from it, as much as he got."

"That boy would eat candy all day if you let him. He's crazy for it. I never give him no money for candy."

"You got the quarter he owes me? You can pay me, an' then he can owe it to you, seein' as he's your son."

"Hell, naw." Coward recoiled slightly. "He ate it all up; he's gotta pay it back. Maybe Tilmon here can take it out of his earnin's."

"Tilmon, can you pay me that quarter? I'm headed to trade, an' I'm gonna need it, seein' as Galloway don't run a line of credit for nobody no more," said Wheeler.

Tilmon took a swig and shook his head. "Don't got no quarter."

"You said you made a good run last month. You didn't make nothin'?" asked Wheeler.

Tilmon shook his head again with his face downcast.

"Hell, Tilmon. What did you do with all that money?"

He gave no answer.

Jason Coward sat back down. "You runnin' a still, Tilmon?"

"Yeah. Still havin' to pay back folks that helped me build it. Took corn on credit and had to pay it with likker, too."

"Did you pay Silas anything yet?" asked Coward.

"Not yet. I'll pay him some after the next run."

Wheeler took another swig and offered the bottle to Coward, who refused with a shake of his head. Wheeler took another swallow before Tilmon retrieved the bottle from him.

"You been stillin' for nearin' a year. You ain't saved nothin'? What're y'all eatin'?"

"I'm growin' some wheat." Tilmon waved the stump of his left arm at the hill where the bright green carpet of grass lay—its brown gashes now impossible not to see.

"Looks more like you're drinkin' your profits," said Wheeler.

Coward spoke up. "You keepin' your still quiet? I don't mind Silas workin' with you on it. Just part of life up here, but Charlie Rogers said that your lawyer neighbor up there was gonna rat you out. Silas don't need no trouble, seein' as he's already got one hand tied behind his back in life." Coward realized too late that he had misspoken.

Tilmon's face flashed red, and he jumped up and pushed Coward backward with his one hand that still held the bottle. "You makin' fun at me?"

Coward grabbed the bottle and held it tightly as Tilmon wobbled a bit. "No. I'm sorry. That was just a figure of speech, ya know. Somethin' you just say. I'm real sorry 'bout that. An' I really appreciate you takin' on Silas for work. I do."

Tilmon sat down and took another drink. "Dang Ratbag."

"Hey now, I said I didn't mean nothin' by it," said Coward.

"Not you."

The front door opened, and Annie peered out at the group. From the look on her face, it was apparent that she had made a correct estimation of the situation. "Tilmon, remember I need you to go over to Galloway's." She shook her head and slammed the door.

Wheeler watched the situation with some amusement. "Tilmon, gimme that bottle. You don't need no more of that this morning." He peeled the bottle from his hand. "We need to go inside, Tilmon. Too cold out here."

Osborne Seay came up the path from the branch, headed in the direction of his father-in-law's house.

"Gentlemen," he said in greeting as he approached the group. "Everybody doin' all right this morning'?"

Wheeler chuckled, "Yeah, might be time for Tilmon here to go back to bed."

Coward introduced himself. "Jason Coward." The men shook.

"Os Seay."

"Come over from Rabun to collect Silas and head over to my sister's."

"Well, nice to meet you," Os said. "Headed over to my father-in-law's house over there." He pointed in the direction of the field, beyond which was Charlie Rogers' place."

"I stayed with Mr. Rogers last night," said Coward.

"Yeah, that's him."

"Come on, let's go sit inside to warm this one up," Wheeler said as he guided a wobbling Justice toward the door.

Os followed the group and was the last to mount the steps to the porch and go inside. Something up in the field caught his eye, and he squinted as he looked up the hill. "Tilmon, looks like you got a sheep walkin' through your field up there." He chuckled. "What's that you got planted up there? Is that wheat? Whatever it is, it's getting trampled."

Tilmon shook Wheeler's hand from his arm and ran out to the corner of the house, where he could see the entire field. "*Aaargh!*" he screamed. He stripped his hat from his head and threw it down, then ran back in with a look of fury. He mounted the porch and ducked past the others into the house. Just a moment later, he came out with the shotgun in one hand, and the satchel of ammunition slung over his shoulder.

"Come on with me, let's go run out that sheep." Tilmon stumbled down the steps and motioned to Coward as he took off around the other end of the house and down the path toward the branch, staggering slightly as he ran.

"What the hell?" asked Wheeler.

"He's drunk as Cooter Brown, sure enough. Shouldn't somebody go after him?" asked Coward.

"Help yourself," said Wheeler. "This ought to be good."

"This don't look like it'll be good at all," said Coward.

"Oh, he'll calm down in a minute. I've seen him lit up before," said Os.

Coward looked at the two younger men uncertainly, waiting for one of them to come with him, but they didn't seem concerned. Only Coward followed, and he got winded quickly chasing down the trail after the much younger man. As he approached, he called, "Tilmon." He caught up and put a hand on Tilmon's shoulder. "Wait a minute. This way don't go up to your field."

Tilmon pulled his shoulder away. "He'd better wear glasses if he's gon' go lookin' for my still. He's gettin' ready to be lookin' down the barrel of this gun," said Tilmon.

Just as they rounded a thicket, they met up with Old Man Godard on the path. He didn't see them immediately with his hat pulled down tightly onto his head. He was stabbing and two-stepping along the path with a stick in one hand—the other stuffed tightly down into the pocket of his grey wool coat. A long shock of white whiskers fanned out in front of the coat like a lace collar. Thick mud coated his shoes, and there were tiny green shoots stuck in the seams at the soles. When he finally looked up, he glared at Tilmon.

"Get out of my way," said the old man.

With the gun still hanging at his side, Tilmon cocked one of the barrels with his thumb. "Did you go an' say somethin'?"

Godard's look of disdain softened slightly. "About what?" He looked back and forth quizzically between Coward and Justice. "Say something about what?"

Tilmon put the barrel of the gun over the crook of his left elbow and nestled it into the fleshy knob. He took a step forward. He raised his left shoulder, pulling the weapon awkwardly in front of him to point the barrel toward the old man.

Godard looked slightly panicked and stepped back. As he pulled his right hand out of his pocket, a five-dollar bill fell out and fluttered down to the mud. Both of the men stopped to look, but when Justice saw the piece of paper, he scowled and seemed to get even more irritated.

"Trampling my crop is takin' food offa my table, but messin' with a man's business is worse."

Godard's resolve returned as he raised his voice. "You planted on my land. Mine! Your stillin' is illegal, and you are corrupting that fool boy and leading him into a life of crime with you. I'm goin' to Galloway's. Get out of my way!" He waved the cane at Justice like it was a sword as he took a step forward to retrieve the money from the ground.

Tilmon repositioned the shotgun as he put his foot on the green and black piece of paper lying in the mud between them.

"You're not gonna shoot me—you can't even aim that thing with one arm."

This put Tilmon over the edge, and his drink-fueled fury reached its zenith. He was purple with rage as he leveled the gun at him and moved forward step by step, slowly backing Godard up the path and into the bushes.

"Tilmon? Tilmon!" said Godard with rising panic as he retreated up the hill.

"What are you doing, Tilmon?" asked Coward urgently.

"Say anything, and I'll kill you, too," said Justice, without breaking his stare into the eyes of the old man.

Coward stayed put—horrified by the scene but paralyzed with fear—as the two men moved out of sight, further up the path and deeper into the bushes. Eventually, he could no longer see either of them.

The back and forth between the men continued in words that Coward could no longer make out, Godard's voice an indistinct whimper as Justice growled. Then there was a pause. Maybe this was all over. Coward opened his mouth to call out, but before he could say anything, the deafening blast jolted him. Someone screamed. Just a few seconds later, the gun fired again. He took a step forward, peering up the path from around the bush, but he couldn't see what was going on. Sounds of a struggle. Two short cries. Pounding thuds.

Silence.

Coward held his breath for a long moment. As he exhaled, he suddenly noticed the fog from his breath, and he realized that he was trembling. Even his bones felt cold.

Ten or fifteen steps up the path, Tilmon stepped out of the thicket without the gun. Tiny flecks of blood covered his face and coat. There was blood on his hand. He walked silently toward Coward, then stopped and picked up the five-dollar note. He contemplated it for a moment before he wiped it off on his sleeve and stuffed it into his pants pocket, then he marched past Coward toward the branch twenty yards below.

Coward followed. "You didn't kill him, did you?"

"I guess he won't ever rat on anybody else." Tilmon knelt on a flat rock at the edge of the stream and washed his hand in the water. He wiped his face, then dried his hand on the front of his coat as he stood.

Tilmon turned and glared with fury at Coward. He took a step closer. Coward could feel the hot drunk breath on his face as Tilmon leaned forward and said with a malevolent sneer, "If you ever tell anybody, I'll kill you." In the next moment, it was as if he had turned into another person, and just as though nothing had ever happened, he said, "Come on. Let's go get Silas."

Chapter Ten

Tuesday, January 18, 1887

Tilmon groaned as Isaac and Lura climbed on the bed with him and badgered him to get up. He had a splitting headache. He had not heard Annie at all. She was already in the front room, cleaning up the breakfast dishes. When he finally appeared, she didn't speak. It was always this way after a particularly bad spell with the corn, but Tilmon couldn't remember having drunk that much before. He sat at the table and drank two big glasses of water, then put his head down on his hand. His ears were ringing.

"Can I have some grits?" he asked.

"No more. Gave them all to the kids. I didn't get any, neither. I asked you to go to Galloway's yesterday," said Annie tersely.

"I'm sorry. I'll go today."

With no reply, she went into the other room and began to make the bed.

Tilmon put on his coat and boots and went outside to tend to the mare. A heavy frost covered the ground. When he got to the shed, he was dismayed to find that the horse was still saddled and bridled and had spent the night without the blanket over her. He removed the horse tack and put the blanket over her back, then pulled out some hay from the loft and threw it in the bin for her to feed. He went to the trough and got her a bucket of water after he busted up the ice on the surface.

Yesterday was just a blur. He looked up in the field and vaguely remembered walking around up there in pursuit of the turkeys. His head was pounding, and he felt terrible. He looked up on the shelf for his bottle. Not there. He looked all around in the shed. No bottle. Suddenly the mare kicked out and struck the nearby bucket. The loud sound startled him, and he winced. It reminded him of a gunshot and brought vague worries of something terrible—ominous, unclear, nauseating. He felt the urge to vomit and stepped to the side of the shed where he retched. *Where is that damned bottle?* Back up at the house, he found the flask bottle that he kept tucked into the eaves of the porch. It had less than an inch in the bottom, but he took it all in one swallow, then leaned against the door awaiting the relief.

A small, muscular man, bundled up against the cold, appeared on the path and called to him. "Hey, Tilmon. How you doin'?" Abner Holden was the young sheriff who lived down further toward Titus. He didn't usually come up to the Settlement. He was a sober man, but was liked by everyone, always available to help out where he could. He took his job seriously, and didn't ever smile much, so the concerned look on his face today was just about his usual and was no cause for worry.

"Fine all right. You?" he replied unconvincingly. Tilmon stepped from the porch and sat down on the step. "What are you up here for?"

"Rogers sent me. Said you borrowed the gun yesterday, and I wanted to get it to go huntin' today. Can I have it?"

Tilmon recalled having the gun in the upper field, and then he remembered having it down by the branch when he was with Coward; then, a vision of him shooting the gun flashed into his brain. The memories of yesterday came back to him gradually, in pieces, like fragments of a broken mirror, offering an imperfect image and jagged interruptions. Pieces of something ugly, of something bad.

"Turkey. I was huntin' a turkey," Tilmon said with his head in his hand. "They was turkeys up in my wheat."

"Did you get you one? A tom or a hen?"

Tilmon couldn't respond. *What?* He didn't really remember.

"A tom," he said absently. He just wanted the conversation to end. He wanted his headache to go away. He wanted to be somewhere else and to be left alone.

"Nice. Was he big? Good eatin', I'd 'spect?"

"Um, yeah. Real big."

"Were you close enough to bring him down with the first shot?"

Will you just get on out of here? I don't know. "Yeah, fluttered like hell."

"I came down around your field just now, an' I didn't see no signs of 'em. You see 'em regular up around there?"

Tilmon didn't respond.

"Did you tack his beard up?" Abner looked across the front of the porch eaves and the porch rail for the shock of black, hair-like feathers from the front breast of a male turkey that hunters usually hung by the front door. There was no trophy to be seen.

"Let me get that gun for ya'," Tilmon said, finally working his way to his feet, eager to get this visitor on his way. As he stood to go in the house, another piece of yesterday flashed through his mind. *A beard. Godard!* He saw the old man's face in a foggy recollection. He stopped with his back to Holden and leaned against the post.

"Tilmon? You gonna go get that gun?"

He suddenly knew that he didn't have the gun anymore, but he didn't remember where it was. "I just remembered," he stammered and turned around, "I gave that gun to Osborne Seay. Said he needed it. Maybe go on up to his place." *Will you please just go?* Tilmon remembered washing his hand in the branch. He looked at his dirty hand. There was blood under his fingernails.

"Good morning, gentlemen," said Pastor Eller, coming up the path from the direction of the church.

Holden and Eller exchanged greetings and looked uncomfortably at each other. Tilmon just nodded. They stared at him. He felt sick. "Where you headed?" he finally asked the preacher.

"Pretty sad day. Goin' down to the branch. Word is, a man was murdered down there yesterday; gonna go see about it," he said.

In a flash, all the pieces came together. The ruined field, the fury, the running, the gun—it all came crashing down on him. He suddenly felt dizzy and sat back down on the stoop. Holden and Eller remained silent as they stared blankly at him.

He shook his head slightly. "What is our country coming to?" said Tilmon. He couldn't look them in the face but stared away up at his field in the distance. Stripes of beautiful pale green with ugly brown gashes running down the hill.

"Tilmon, can you come with us?" asked Holden.

It was then that Tilmon realized. They knew—they already knew.

He nodded. "Give me a minute, will ya?" He went inside. Somber-faced, Annie got up from the table and turned away from him, busying herself at the larder. Tilmon went into the back room. He picked up the only book in the whole house and laid it on the bed, then he reached into his front pocket and pulled out the piece of paper. The bill was muddy and crumpled. He laid it on the Bible and tried to flatten it out, but the creases were impressed with dirt and blood. He wiped it off as best he could and put it inside the cover, then replaced the book on the table in the corner.

When he returned, the three men took the path down toward the branch. They walked slowly and silently. As they neared a clearing halfway to the church, they passed a group of ladies departing the area. Walking three abreast, the red-haired woman in the middle was sobbing and wiping her eyes as she leaned on the others for support.

"Over here, Tilmon," said Holden as they reached a place where the path diverged. "This way." He pointed at the narrow, less-traveled path around the thicket.

Tilmon followed, lifting a low branch, ducking past it. Ten more steps, then ten more.

In a clearing, Charlie Rogers turned to see them approach. David Parker and James Parker were there. Osborne Seay. Jonathan Nicholson. The men all turned and looked at Tilmon without a word. Fifteen feet behind them, it was there, clad in a grey coat, covered with blood. Long grey whiskers fluttered in the breeze as though mocking him by waving a greeting.

Tilmon turned away and suddenly went weak in the knees. Pastor Eller took his arm and helped him sit down on a fallen log. Tilmon put his head in his hand with his back to the group. In a minute, another piece of memory returned, and he reached under the log and slid his hand along the bottom edge. There was nothing there. A wave of nausea overtook him, and he vomited.

Abner Holden finally spoke. "Tilmon Justice, you are suspicioned of murder, and I came to find you today to arrest you for it. Do you have any objection to that?"

"I reckon not."

Chapter Eleven

Tuesday, February 1, 1887

The Clarkesville jail, south of Hiawassee in Habersham County, was the best place for the worst criminals, so the neighboring counties sent their prisoners there to await trial. Keeping the accused there, more distant from the scene of an alleged crime, also had the benefit of helping to avoid a more immediate but less dutiful administration of justice that a lynching would provide. That type of expedited punishment, doled out at the hands of a mob without due process, was a real risk for the three accused murderers being held there, but even more so for the two black men locked up with them. One of the Negroes had been caught stealing a cow, and the other had been jailed on the accusation of stealing just forty cents—a charge he consistently denied.

The party that brought Justice to the jail left Hiawassee in the late afternoon and arrived in Clarkesville long after dark. Two armed deputies on horseback accompanied the small wagon bearing Tilmon Justice, who had his single hand cuffed to a bolt on its floor and his feet tied together for the forty-mile trip. When they arrived at the sheriff's house, they were directed around to the back by the woman who answered the door. A few minutes later, the guards frog-marched Justice into the kitchen by lamplight.

"Over here," said the local jailer, A. J. Crane, as he pulled a lever hanging from the ceiling and led them through another door into the brick structure built onto the back of the house. Down a short hallway, Crane unlocked the first cell with a big key and slid the iron bars to the side. He kicked at the bottom bunk where another inmate was sleeping, curled up under a blanket with his face to the wall.

"What?" asked the man, rolling over to look up at the posse and squinting at the light from the lantern that Crane held aloft.

The guards shoved Tilmon into the tiny cell. "This man's goin' on the bottom bunk," said Crane.

"I was here first," said the inmate sharply.

"Do what you're told," said Crane, with another kick to the bunk. "This man's in that bunk 'cause I said so, an' that's all you need to know. He's only got one arm and pro'lly can't climb up top there."

Tilmon did nothing to correct the jailer's underestimation.

The first man glowered at his new cellmate as he climbed into the top bunk, dragging one of the blankets with him. Crane slid the door shut and turned the key, and the posse went back into the kitchen. With a grating sound in the ceiling, a sliding bar secured the cell doors shut as someone slid the lever back to the locked position.

The next morning, Tilmon was able to survey his surroundings more fully. Three tiny, barred windows, each opposite one of the three cells sitting side by side, were the only source of light for the small brick building. Sliding bars faced the hallway, and brick walls separated the cells. The man in the upper bunk was still snoring away when Tilmon sat up with a groan and put his feet on the floor. There was no heat. He wrapped the blanket around his shoulders.

"You awake over there?" asked a voice from the next cell.

"Yeah. What's your name?"

"Morris, yours?"

"Tilmon Justice."

"Oh yeah. Read about you in the paper. You killed that man who ratted on you to the revenuers?"

"So they say. Innocent until proven guilty, last I checked. You? Why you in here?"

Morris chuckled. "Revenuer came upon my rig at the wrong time, an' he got 'imself killed all right. I didn't do that neither. Waitin' on an appeal to Governor Gordon."

"Who else is in here?"

"Two more boys on the other side a me? Thievin'. Both of 'em."

From farther down, a voice of a grown black man protested. "I didn't do no stealin', an' I ain't gon' confess to somethin' I didn't do, no way."

Tilmon's cellmate awakened with the conversation. "What's your name?"

"Tilmon Justice."

"I'm Sisk. What have they got you in here for?"

"They say I done murder, but I got me a lawyer. Hell, I had to sign my whole farm over to them 'fore they took me down here, so I sure as hell better not get convicted."

* * *

The days passed slowly, torturing Tilmon with thoughts of home and worry about what would happen to his family. They'd had no money to begin with, but without any income, Annie and the kids would be reliant on the help of family and friends. This alone saddened him, but even more so because Annie would be ashamed of it. That humiliation was enough to bring tears to a man. Then he'd lay awake through the night wondering about what was going to happen with the trial. He didn't really remember killing Godard, but with the little pieces he could recollect, he knew that he'd done it—and he knew that he'd hang for it—unless he could somehow get free. Escape was the only solution. *If I can just get out of here. We need to get to somewhere we can make a new start, maybe. I know them woods good, an' I can get us all out west somewhere. Now how can I get out of this here jail?*

He began to think and plan. For more than two weeks, Justice watched the routines and learned more about his cellmates. Twice each day, the jailer wheeled in meager meals in tin plates on a rickety wooden cart. The prisoners ate on their bunks. The men—no one could remember the last time they'd kept a woman in the jail—pissed in jugs and were escorted in leg irons to the outhouse in the walled yard once each day.

From the end of his bunk, Justice had a partial view of the door leading into the sheriff's kitchen, and sometimes he could see or hear a little of what went on inside. He had nothing else to do—he couldn't read a book even if they'd provided one, so for two weeks, he watched, and he studied the mechanism of the locks and the sliding bar.

"Hey Sisk, you gotta piece of string?" he asked after memorizing the mealtime routine.

"What fer?"

"I could loop it around the end of the latch inside the lock here an' keep it tied up, so when the key turns over, the latch don't fall."

"So?"

"So, then whenever the top bar is back, you could slide the door open without the key."

"So?"

"So, when they pull the bar, we could get out before they unlockin' the door."

From the middle cell, Morris spoke up. "Yeah, I got it. Since Crane starts down here to bring the boys their plates first, that gives us a chance. I got part of a shoelace. I could fix it up on my door."

84

"No," replied Justice. You gotta tie it up while the door is pulled open, but with nobody watchin'. Takes two hands an' you gotta be quick. I need Sisk here to do it when they takin' me to th' outhouse."

Morris passed the broken piece of shoelace through the bars and around the wall to Justice, who took it and knelt on the floor. He peered into the side of the locking mechanism behind the protective plate on the bars of the sliding door.

Justice motioned for Sisk to look and pointed out the flaw in the design.

"See there," he said, "if you fix a little loop in this string, next time the door is open, you'n hook aroun' that lever an' fix it up to that bar there. Then the latch can't fall when he pulls the door an' turns the key."

Sisk studied the design and nodded. "The ceiling bar locks us in at the top, but the next time they pull the bar, we'n slide the door right then."

"When I call to go out to the privy, I'll block his view and make you some time so you can fix up the latch," said Tilmon.

"What about me?" asked Morris.

"We'll get the key from the jailer and let y'all out. But when we run, every man is on his own," said Tilmon.

"Fine by me," said Morris. "What about you down there?" Morris called to the men in the far cell. "You goin' with us?"

"If this door opens, I'm going out it," said one, but the other man remained silent.

"All right then. I'm going to call to go out, and I'll distract 'em so Sisk can fix it up. Ready?"

Justice hollered out for the guard. "Hey! I gotta go out to the yard." There was no immediate response, so he called again. "Guard! Sheriff! I gotta go out."

Crane came in from the door at the end of the hall. "You went this mornin' after breakfast. Why you gotta go now?"

"That greasy breakfast is why I gotta go now,' said Tilmon. "Guts been rumbling all mornin'. You better let me go, I tell you, or it's gonna be a problem."

"Problem for you, not for me," said Crane.

"I can't do nothing 'bout it, but I tell you, it's positively un-Christian of you not to have mercy on a man wi' his bowels in an uproar."

Crane shook his head and sighed. "All right, gimme a minute. Lemme get the keys." He went back into the house and pulled the lever, sliding the ceiling bar forward, returning with the keys and a shotgun. He leaned the gun against the wall opposite the cell, took a set of manacles from the adjacent hook, then reached through the bars to put them on Tilmon's legs. He retrieved the gun before he unlocked the cell door and slid it to the side.

Tilmon shuffled forward, standing between Crane and the lock mechanism. He put his hand on his belly and grimaced as he groaned.

"Got bad cramps," he said, leaning against the bars to obscure Crane's view of Sisk and the exposed lock plate.

Sitting on the bunk behind them, Sisk leaned forward to put the loop on the latch and tied it up inside the lock so that the mechanism couldn't function.

"Make it snappy. We ain't got all day here," Crane said. He pulled the door shut, turning and withdrawing the key in a single, practiced maneuver. "Come on then," he said, grabbing the inmate's collar with one hand, his shotgun tucked under his other arm at the ready. Tilmon continued to feign discomfort as he shuffled out through the door.

Twenty minutes later, the men returned, and with the reverse process, Crane secured Tilmon back in the cell—or so he thought.

Sisk glanced at Tilmon, raised his eyebrows, and gave a slight nod.

While Crane hung up the manacles and walked back toward the door to the house, Tilmon pulled against the door to the cell to test his idea. It slid open. He pushed it quickly back to the closed position, just before the overhead bar slid back into place and locked them inside. That night Tilmon, Sisk, and Morris made plans for their escape.

At noon the next day, Crane pulled the bar and brought five dinner plates in on a cart, each laden with potatoes, field peas, and cornbread. The food smelled unusually good, and the men were surprised to see that the peas were cooked with bacon.

Crane unlocked and opened the door, passed two tin plates into the first cell, then pulled the door shut. He apparently didn't notice anything unusual about the lock.

"Ready?" Sisk whispered.

"Wait," replied Tilmon. The cart moved down to the next cell, and Morris got his dinner. "Let's get dinner first. Might be a while 'til we eat again."

After passing all the plates, Crane left the cart at the end of the row and went back into the house, sliding the bar in place behind him.

The inmates ate hungrily, then finalized their plan.

Justice spoke to Morris, "He'll be back in a few minutes. When he slides open your door, Sisk and I can rush out and grab him; then we'll have three on one."

"We gon' kill 'im?" asked Morris.

"No need," said Justice. "Just take the gun an' the key an' lock 'im in."

"You gon' let us out?" asked the cow thief from the farthest cell.

"Yeah, we'll unlock you, but then you're on your own," said Morris.

"I din' take no forty cent, an' I ain't gon' run no ways, or th' judge gon' say I done it fer sure," said the other black man.

"Up to you then, but if you say a word when the jailer comes, I'll kill you before I leave," said Morris. "I got nothin' to lose."

"I don' know nuffin', I don' say nuffin'," said the black man.

"Shh. Here he comes," said Justice as the ceiling bar slid back to release the doors.

Crane came in, jangling the ring of keys in his hand. At the end of the corridor, he put the shotgun on the cart, unlocked the door of the Negroes' cell, retrieved the plates then turned the key back the other way to secure the lock. At the middle cell, as Crane unlocked the door and pulled it aside, Justice heard the tin pan hit the floor, then saw Morris crash into the jailer, pushing him outside against the wall. In an instant, Justice slid open the door to their cell, and Sisk piled onto the fight with Justice right behind. The three men pinned the jailer down—Morris knelt on his chest and secured one arm, and Sisk sat on the other. He grabbed the gun and pointed it at his head, keeping a hand clamped over Crane's mouth. Justice grabbed the keys.

"Say a word, and I'll kill you right here," said Sisk. Crane quit struggling and nodded in agreement, wide-eyed with fear.

With the gun trained on the lawman, Justice and Morris dragged him into the middle cell, slid the door closed, and locked it. Then Justice unlocked the far cell so the cattle thief could join them.

"My daughter is in the kitchen," said Crane. "Don't hurt her."

"Don't make a sound, and we won't," said Sisk, backing down the hallway.

When Morris opened the door to the house, he saw another officer there, apparently oblivious to what had just transpired only a few feet away. Morris swung immediately, landing an uppercut that left the man unconscious on the floor, then he grabbed the pistol from the lawman's belt, and they dragged him into the first cell. They left him on the floor and slid the door closed. Before they moved on, the cattle thief pushed the ceiling lever to secure the cell doors, trapping Crane and the other jailer inside. Now armed with two guns, the four escapees ran down the hall and into the kitchen, where they found Crane's daughter working, unaware. She shrieked and dropped a bowl to shatter on the floor when she saw them.

"Don't say a word," said Morris, leveling the pistol on her. "Git us out of here, and we won't hurt ya." The teenager cowered behind the table, clutching her apron over her face, and pointed down another hall toward an exterior door. They grabbed some vittles as they passed and shoved them in their pockets. Justice pocketed a small knife.

With his foot firmly lodged against it for protection, Sisk cracked open the kitchen door to peek outside and survey their escape route.

"It's clear. Let's go," he said.

The four ducked out the door and hurried three blocks out of town, headed straight for the woods. They didn't run, but this unusual and unkempt band of four—including an Negro and a one-armed man—brandishing weapons as they hurried nervously away from the jail, was far from innocent-looking and sure to attract attention.

Two blocks north of the train depot, they crossed the tracks and headed into the woods, only stopping to rest when they were well out of view.

"This is where we split up," said Morris.

"Where you headed?" asked Sisk.

"Don't know. Pro'lly east," he replied.

"Halt!"

They turned with alarm toward the voice of a lone man calling to them. "Halt! Stay where you are and drop your weapons. You're all under arrest."

Morris called back. "Keep away if you know what's good for ya'!" He fired a pistol shot in the direction of the pursuer but missed badly—the man ducked and retreated toward the tracks behind him.

"Good luck, then," said Sisk.

The men went their separate ways. Morris ran off toward the south, Sisk and the cow thief ran north, and Justice sprinted east toward the hills in the distance as the voices of an assembling posse arose near the train station.

* * *

Two days later, he was still running.

What was that?

He'd spent his whole life in these mountains, but every little sound or movement in his peripheral vision startled him so that he froze still to listen and watch. He knew that staying perfectly still in a good hiding place would keep him unseen, even if his pursuers were very close by. Though sound didn't carry too far, even the slightest movement attracted attention. Nevertheless, he had to keep moving. He couldn't just hide forever.

So tired. I need to lie down.

There was no trouble finding places for cover when he needed to rest—in a cleft of a rock formation, behind a fallen log, or deep inside a thicket of mountain laurels like where he'd have set up a still. Nevertheless, he was exhausted. The anxiety and the constant vigilance that it required were taking their toll.

I could use a drink.

The first few days in jail were hell. Not just the worry, but the headaches and the tremors and the retching. That abated after three days or so, but now his stomach hurt from hunger. The biscuits and bacon he'd snagged from the kitchen at the jailhouse were distant memories. As he'd eaten the last bite, he wondered when he would ever have a biscuit again.

He watched a cabin from a distance for hours. It was occupied—he could tell by the smoke from the chimney, but he didn't see any one around. People would generally share something if asked, but word would be out about a one-armed man who had escaped from jail.

Can't lie. One arm sure to give me away.

He snuck up the hill toward the chimney side of the cabin, hoping that his approach would be less visible from the window or the porch. After crossing the remnants of last year's garden, still laying fallow, he ducked behind the small smoke house where he sat down to rest and listen. After several minutes of silence, save for the occasional chirping of a bird, he peeked around the corner, then slowly made his way around to the door. He turned the wooden latch and pulled it open slightly. The door creaked with a noise that startled him after the near total silence of the last two days. He opened it a little more, then stepped inside. After his eyes adjusted to the darkness he confirmed—there was nothing.

I just need to find the river. Which way do I go from here?

Cold, grey skies obscured the sun, complicating navigation as he climbed up and down the hills, keeping off the roads for the most part and taking the trails he thought were running north and east. If he could intercept the river, he ought to be able to reorient himself.

Who's gonna harvest my wheat? Godard! Dang ratbag!

He hadn't been able to make a fire—didn't have any matches nor a flint.

I need to find a place out of the wind. Hope it don't snow.

Thoughts of home and his family drove him on, but he wondered how well he'd be received by his neighbors. Would he have to sneak back into the Settlement?

Wonder will the folks in the Settlement turn me in? Dang Abner Holden.

We'll all head up to North Carolina and disappear. I could keep goin', I guess. Maybe I should go over to Tennessee.

Would Annie be able to go, even if she were willing to leave?

She ain't gonna leave her family.

We'll have to walk.

Lura can't walk that far, and I'm gonna have to carry her.

Annie couldn't walk that far—she'd be having the baby soon.

What if she heads north with me and then goes into labor on the way? I seen the midwife deliver a baby; I could do that. Could I do that with just one hand? Maybe she already had the baby? What will we eat? She'll have to have enough food if she's going to be able to nurse the baby. Here's a road. Is this the road to the Settlement? It's gonna be dark soon.

He realized that the creek he was following was running west. He needed to be going north and east.

No, wait. This is going the wrong way. I need to lie down.

"Tilmon Justice, you hold it right there, or I'll drop you dead," said the lawman. The posse saw him as he worked his way to the ground using a tree for support. Tilmon was so delirious from hypothermia and hunger and exhaustion that the hadn't even heard them coming up the hill behind him.

Chapter Twelve

TUESDAY, SEPTEMBER 27, 1887

Of the nearly 4000 people who lived in Towns County, the city of Hiawassee was home to only 600 of them—by and large, they were the folks who had a little bit of money. As the county seat, it was the hub for business and commerce—a growing city, with hopes to build a train stop for a planned rail line across the northern tier of the state. In the city, the more cosmopolitan people in the area could attend one of six different churches scattered across the valley; they had schools to attend, shops to visit, and businesses to work in. On its periphery, smaller farms provided for the city dwellers, but the rest of the county's population lived out in the near country or further out in the wilderness by choice or by requirement and eked out a meager existence as subsistence farmers, traders, and loggers—and moonshiners.

The courthouse, at the corner of Lee and River Streets in Hiawassee, was a long two-story building with a portico on the end and symmetrical external staircases leading to the courtroom doors on the second floor. On the long sides of the building, three tall chimneys stuck up from the roof at intervals, capped by wisps of smoke that curled into the sky and disappeared in the wind. In anticipation of the trial, the county had completed some renovations on the building this year. Judge Carlos J. Wellborn surveyed the building with a sense of pride as he walked in. As bad as this situation was, he had been able to leverage it for the benefit of the courthouse. The commissioners had pushed for the improvements, expecting a capacity crowd and lots of attention—the murder case having become a sensation in newspapers nationwide. A dozen men in the community made twenty-thousand new shingles for the roof, and new iron braces had been placed beneath the floors and under the attic to reinforce and support the walls. Fresh paint covered every surface.

The judge was an esteemed father of the community. After his many years on the bench, the citizens of Towns County could always depend on Judge Wellborn to deliver even-handed and circumspect decisions; he frequently took the opportunity to teach and admonish, and he demonstrated kindness when appropriate to the situation. The judge knew several of the parties involved in this trial. He'd levied several fines against Mr. Godard for his involvement in selling liquor on Sunday back when he lived in town, and he'd had to adjudicate a nasty fight between Godard and one of his neighbors— where neither party had been innocent. Mr. Coward had some his run-ins with the law over in Rabun County, and Tilmon Justice was a familiar man in town. Judge Wellborn was concerned about how the verdict of this trial would affect everyone involved—including himself. *What if the jury returned a guilty verdict?* The stress of the first trial, with all the bickering and the rancor that developed between the jurors, and the misbehavior among the attorneys, as well as the press and the public pressure in the intervening months had taken its toll. Wellborn hadn't slept well and had spent many hours alone with his thoughts as the second trial approached. His wife seemed to understand that he needed this time, and she kept visitors and the newspapermen at bay.

The second trial of Justice was to start in the afternoon after months of delays. This morning, the jurors had been selected during the voire dire, when the attorneys took turns interviewing the potential participants in alternating rounds of questions. Sometimes they excused the prospective juror without much ado, and it only took two hours to select the twelve men and six alternates. All the jurors were from Towns County, and all of them had heard of the case. Many of them knew someone involved, and a few of them had relatives from up in the Settlement, but none of them had been participants in the first trial—nor were they kin to anyone who had.

Before lunch, Judge Wellborn called the attorneys in his chambers, and behind closed doors, he chastised them for an hour before the start of the proceedings, reinforcing his control over the process and their conduct. The first trial in April had ended with a hung jury, and he didn't want any of the problems from the previous trial repeated. Wellborn had been the judge then, too, and he just couldn't believe some of the things that had transpired. Newspapermen had followed the jurors home, looking for 'first-hand' accounts of what had gone on in deliberations. There were reports that some of the jurors' family members had been approached by unknown persons who were lobbying for a certain verdict for the trial—though no one had actually used the word 'bribe' to describe those activities. Judge Wellborn had even heard that back-room odds-makers were taking bets on the outcome. One of the jurors held out stubbornly for weeks until Judge Wellborn finally had no choice but to call a mistrial.

When the jury was finally led into the courtroom, seated in the jury box before a table laden with evidence, and with the defendant shackled to his chair nearby, the judge repeated his admonishments for everyone gathered there.

"Gentlemen, good afternoon. Thank you for being here today. In a few moments, we will commence to hear evidence that will allow you to render a verdict on this case which has consumed our county and the whole of this state for nearly a year. One of our citizens is accused of murder, and it's weighed heavily on us all for many months. The last trial did not reflect well on our community, what with the misbehavior I've heard of and a deadlocked jury. This brings us here again today—at great expense to the taxpayers of Georgia and Towns County, mind you." The judge ran a hand across his silver beard and contemplated his notes for a moment. "As we get started, let me reiterate that Mr. Justice is innocent until proven guilty. Your duty is to listen to only the facts presented here and then use that information to come to a verdict. Whatever you've heard before does not matter. What your wife thinks does not matter. What you've read in the newspaper does not matter. You are to keep an open mind and listen to the facts. In the evenings, I will release you to your homes, but you must not discuss anything you've heard in this courtroom, or anything about this case, or the previous trial. I don't need to remind you that idle talk takes on a life of its own and becomes more sensational and fantastic with each retelling, but at the same time, it departs further from the truth." Judge Wellborn inspected the room, peering over his spectacles to meet the eyes of some of the onlookers and add emphasis.

He steeled himself and turned on the attorneys again with a slightly sterner tone. "Gentlemen, I expect you to uphold the highest standards of deportment in my courtroom, and you will all show the utmost in courtesy and respect to every person here. I will not tolerate misbehavior from any of you. Do I make myself clear?" They nodded but didn't dare to meet his eye. Judge Wellborn scanned the fully packed room again to make his point once more. No one stirred.

"Good. Now, we all know why we're here, and we've done this before, so I trust that the opening statements from both the State and the defense will be brief and to the point?" The attorneys looked slightly crestfallen, but, nevertheless, both sides agreed. "Mr. Thompson," said Judge Wellborn, "you may proceed."

The prosecuting attorney—the solicitor general for the area—popped up from his chair at the table where he was seated with his associate.

"Thank you, Your Honor," said Howard Thompson, turning to the room with a bit of a flourish. The portly man was overdressed for a Towns County crowd; he was originally from somewhere down near Atlanta and had always carried himself differently from the locals. He seemed haughty to some and was not well-liked. As he approached the jurors, he straightened his tie and brushed off his lapels.

"Gentlemen, this is quite straightforward in our estimation. The State will show that Mr. Tilmon Justice is guilty of the murder of Mr.

James B. Godard—an esteemed local attorney. The victim and the accused had a dispute over a land boundary that had been ongoing for a number of years. We will call as witnesses some members of the Settlement up on Charlie's Creek, who can attest to this—and to other possible motives that Mr. Justice may have had." Thompson raised an eyebrow knowingly at the jurors, some of whom smirked. Judge Wellborn frowned at the attorney in silent admonition.

Thompson continued. "We will establish that Mr. Justice was in possession of the local shotgun, taken from the home of Mr. Charles Rogers, and you will hear from the man who was nearby as the horrible crime was committed. He will testify that Mr. Godard was traversing the disputed land on that fateful morning and will confirm that Tilmon Justice, in a state of drunkenness, shot Mr. Godard, then..." Thompson punctuated the next four words with a fist to his palm. "Beat. Him. To. Death." Thompson turned to look at the defendant seated just three steps away at the defense table and paused before turning back to the jury. Silently, slowly, he struck his palm with his fist four more times. "Gentlemen, Tilmon Justice had the motive, he had the means, and he had the opportunity to murder Mr. James Godard. Once you are aware of all the facts related to these elements, you will easily be able to find him guilty of murder in the first degree." Thompson spoke to the judge before taking his seat. "That will be all, Your Honor."

Judge Wellborn nodded to the defense attorney seated at the table with the defendant. "Mr. Kimsey, your opening statement, please."

Kimsey was a local boy who had learned his profession by apprenticing around with others until he was acquainted enough with the procedures and processes and people and politics to join up with a group of lawyers practicing in Hiawassee. He was younger and not nearly as polished nor as fancy as the solicitor—his suit and shoes were respectable, but barely. Nevertheless, the young defense attorney was earnest and motivated. He was happy to take the case, though none of the older partners felt he had even the slightest chance of success, and the client had no money. Kimsey convinced the attorneys to take the deed for the parcel of land and the cabin in the Settlement in trade for the defense; and with no other options, Tilmon Justice had reluctantly signed the farmland over to Kimsey and the defense team as payment for his services.

Kimsey rose from his seat beside Tilmon Justice to address the jurors. "Gentlemen, there's no proof that Tilmon Justice killed James Godard. During this trial, you might hear some things that *suggest* he's guilty, but suggesting he done murder ain't enough to convict. That's called circumstantial evidence—things that might make you 'spicious, but don't really prove that Tilmon Justice actually did it. Some people will say they heard some things that was said by summody else. But that's called hearsay. Just sayin' somethin' don't necessarily mean it happened that way. Don't make it true just 'cause you say so. I 'spect you'll hear some things that make you think the defendant is involved in some other kind of business activities—but whatever else Mr. Justice mighta been doin', that don't have nothing to do with this case. Our question for the jury is simple. *Is it possible that there's somebody else who killed Mr. Godard?* Gentlemen, this is a terrible crime. Murder. A person found guilty of a murder like this will surely hang. That makes it all the more critical that your verdict be correct. A guilty verdict can only be made if all of you feel that the defendant is guilty *beyond a reasonable doubt*. Not a doubt in your mind. You got picked to be on this jury because you can think things through. You can weigh the evidence completely an' be impartial. Hearsay and circumstantial evidence is all that they got against Mr. Justice." Kimsey paused and paced the floor in front of the jurors. "It's like this—nobody actually *saw* Tilmon Justice kill Mr. Godard. The prosecution's case is built on supposition, assumption, and conjecture—that means there's no *proof*. If you find him guilty, it has to be 'cause there is no doubt in your mind that nobody but him coulda done it, but you'll see it *is* possible that somebody else killed James Godard." Kimsey nodded to the judge and took his seat, then patted Tilmon on the shoulder.

Judge Wellborn looked at the defendant. Justice wore a fresh shirt and pants for the court appearance. He'd had his hair cut and was clean-shaven in an effort to make a better presentation, but he looked tired. Worn. He held his head in his hand with his face to the floor much of the time, unless prompted by Kimsey's elbow to sit up and to look at the jury. Annie sat just behind Kimsey and her husband. Her face, too, bore a look of such pain, such worry, that one couldn't help but feel for her. She had lost so much weight—from the stress, from having to do with less at home, from having all the work to manage herself, and from feeding the baby that had been born in February while Tilmon was in the Clarkesville jail. Judge Wellborn usually didn't allow children in the courtroom, but the baby needed his mother, and the mother needed to be here. The seven-month-old slept nearly all the time, but when he did cry, Annie pulled her cape around from behind her as a cover while she fed the infant.

"Thank you, gentlemen. The State may call the first witness," said Judge Wellborn as Thompson rose from his chair.

"Your Honor, the State calls Mr. D. L. Parker."

Parker was the young man who had found Godard's body. He stood and came down the aisle to face the bailiff, who proffered a Bible.

"Do you swear to tell the truth, the whole truth and nothing but?"

"I do," said the young man, with one hand on the book and the other in the air, before nervously taking a seat beside the judge's bench.

"Your name is David L. Parker?" asked the prosecutor.

"Yes, sir." He kept his eyes on the floor in front of him.

"And do you know Tilmon Justice, there?" Thompson gestured to the defendant.

"I do," Parker said, glancing up quickly.

"Tell us, when and where did you last see Mr. James Godard alive?"

"On January the 17th. At my daddy's house. In the morning, pretty soon about breakfast."

"He lived near you?"

" 'Bout a mile or so."

"What was he there for?"

"Said he was goin' on to Mr. Galloway's store. Stayed near about an hour, as I can recollect. Left our place about 9 or 10 o'clock."

"Did you have any conversation with Mr. Godard that morning at your house?"

"I don't know that I did."

"Did you hear him say anything about Mr. Justice?"

"No, sir."

"Mr. Parker, did you ever hear Tilmon Justice say anything about being afraid of Godard?"

"No, sir."

"Did you ever hear Mr. Justice make threats against Mr. Godard?"

"One time, when we was up at Mr. Rogers' place..." The young man paused, looking uncertainly at someone in the crowd, as if for reassurance.

"Go on," said Thompson.

In a moment, Parker continued. "Mr. Justice said that if Mr. Godard reported him that he'd kill him."

A slight murmur rippled through the room. Judge Wellborn rapped his gavel on the table twice in a call for silence.

"Who did he say that to?"

"Can't rightly say I know. They was all outside an' they was a good nummer of folks there. I didn't see exactly."

"When was this that you heard Mr. Justice make that threat?"

"Maybe 'bout Christmas eve. Before we went out serenadin'."

"When Mr. Godard left for Galloway's, would he have to go by Justice's house?"

"Yessir. He'd go back by his house, then on down to Justice's. 'Bout a quarter-mile below his."

"On the day of the murder, how long after Godard left your house before you heard the gunshots?"

"Fifteen or twenty minutes. I don't remember exactly."

"Had he been gone long enough to reach Mr. Justice's place?"

"I 'spect so."

"Objection, Your Honor!" Kimsey leaped out of his chair. "That question is just speculation; this witness can't testify to that!"

"Sustained," Judge Wellborn said, glaring over his glasses at Mr. Thompson. "Move on, Counselor."

"Yes, sir," said Thompson flatly. He turned back to the witness. "When you heard the gunshots that morning, what did you think?"

"I said to some of them there at my house that 'Tilmon just killed ol' man Godard.'"

"Why did you have that thought?" asked Thompson.

"I dunno. Just did."

"What did you do after you heard the shots?"

"Well, after a while, me and my brother J. P. went on down to Mr. Justice's place."

"Why were you going down there?"

"I's goin' to see about maybe swappin' some meat and giving him some corn for it."

"But on the way, you found Godard's body?"

"Yes. Near the branch below his house. 'Bout three-hunnert yards from Justice's place."

"And whose land was he on?"

"Tilmon's."

"What was his condition?"

"He was lying on his back, about ten steps off the path. He was in a bad way."

"How so?"

"He was shot up an' his head was beat to a jelly." The room buzzed again as some of the people in the crowd turned to those sitting nearby with serious looks.

Judge Wellborn rapped his gavel lightly. "Quiet, please." Though this testimony had been heard before at the first trial, he knew that the prosecution wanted to make it as sensational as possible to impress the new jury. When the crowd settled down, he motioned for Thompson to continue.

"Did you examine him?" asked Thompson.

"No. We got back to the Settlement and told some folks what we found. Told Mr. Rogers, an' Johnathan Nicholson, an' Elijah Wheeler. Then they went back there with us."

"When you went back, did you find any weapons?"

Parker looked over at the table bearing the evidence. "I saw a gun lock lying by him, an' a big rock."

Mr. Thompson retrieved some items from the table at the front of the room. "Are these them?" He held up the mechanism from a broken shotgun, dangling it from his finger.

"They's the ones we found."

"And this gun?" Thompson held up the broken double barrel.

"No, I don't know that gun, 'cept I think some of the boys found it hid nearby there."

"What about that rock?" He pointed to the stone on the table, as big as an oversized potato, ominously stained dark brown in places.

The judge looked at Tilmon, who had put his elbows on his knees and his face in his hand. Kimsey elbowed the defendant to sit up.

"Yes, that's the rock I found by him."

"Mr. Parker, was it snowing on the day you found the body?"

"No, sir, I think not."

"Can you remember the weather those days?"

"We'd had some rain before, then came a hard freeze for a couple of days after the murder."

"So, the ground was soft on the day you found the body?"

"Yessir. Real muddy."

"Did you see any tracks around the body?"

"They was two sets of tracks on th' path, an' it seemed like there was a right smart bit of scufflin' there, and a place where it seems that Mr. Godard's toes was stuck in the ground."

"But up near the body, what about there?"

"I saw one track leading over to the body, then went away from it."

"Did you follow it?"

"No ways, hardly."

"What size shoe was it?"

"About a number eight, maybe."

Kimsey popped up from his seat at the table next to Justice. "Objection, Your Honor. This is jus' speculation by Mr. Parker."

"Sustained," said Judge Wellborn as he spoke to the jurors, "Please disregard this young man's assessment of the shoe size." He knew, though, that once the words had been said, there was no way the jury could fail to remember them.

Thompson continued with his line of questioning.

"And can you tell me anything more about that track?"

"Well, they's some tacks on the bottom of the shoe."

"Did it impress you as being the track of any certain person?"

Kimsey stood again quickly to address the bench. "Objection, Your Honor. This is more speculation."

"Sustained," said Judge Welborn. "Mr. Thompson, please just keep to the facts."

The prosecutor nodded, then turned back to the witness. "Do you know, did Tilmon Justice's shoes have tacks on the bottom of the sole?"

"Yes, sir. He had a pair that did."

"And finally, Mr. Parker, let me ask you this. Did you see Tilmon Justice that morning?"

Parker hesitated.

"Did you?"

"Yes, I saw him from a distance when we's going down there. He was on the path goin' up to Mr. Godard's house."

"Thank you, Mr. Parker." Thompson addressed the judge. "That will be all at this time, Your Honor."

The judge turned to the defense attorney who was already rising from his chair. "Mr. Kimsey, you may cross-examine the witness."

The defense attorney started in on Parker without any niceties. His voice carried an edge of skepticism. "Did you actually *see* Mr. Justice shoot Mr. Godard?"

"No sir."

"So, it is possible that someone else committed the murder— "

"Objection, Your Honor!" piped Mr. Thompson, jumping to his feet from behind the prosecution table.

"Sustained," Judge Wellborn said as he glared at Mr. Kimsey over his glasses. "That is a question for the jury. Move on."

"Yes, Your Honor," replied Mr. Kimsey. He addressed Parker again. "In December, when you said that there was a threat made, you were not even present, were you?"

"Well, I was inside, and they's a group of men talking down in the yard by the woodpile."

"But you did not actually hear Mr. Justice threaten Mr. Godard."

"Well, there was talk about it after he said so."

"Now, you already said you weren't present there—so you can't be certain that it was Mr. Justice who said that."

"Well, I know—"

"Yes. I know you can't say it for sure 'cause you weren't actually right there, I understand," Kimsey continued before Parker could say anything more, then changed topics. "Are you aware that there is a still house up on the branch where Godard and Justice lived?"

"Yes, I think there was one up there."

Mr. Thompson arose from the prosecution table. "Objection, Your Honor. This line of questioning is not relevant to the case at all."

"Your Honor, this information helps to show that there are others who had a motive to kill Mr. Godard," said Kimsey, looking over at the jury. "These facts are critical to the defense."

"I'll allow it," said the judge.

"Mr. Parker, how long have you been acquainted with Mr. Jason Coward?" asked Kimsey.

"I didn't know him at all till this here happenings."

"Doesn't he live in Rabun?"

"I don't know, but I think he does."

"And you know his boy, Silas?"

"I seen him around."

"Regarding this alleged threat against Godard—which we now know you are not able to definitely say came from Justice—what was it about?"

"Said he was gonna kill him if he reported him."

"Report him for what."

Parker paused momentarily. "I don't know that he said, exactly."

"Is it not true that there was a still house up there by Tilmon's house?"

"I know there was one runnin' right close by there."

"I believe you said that Silas Coward had been living up there in that still house."

"No, sir. I never said that," said Parker, now with a little courage. "I said that I saw him passing around there."

"But you know he was working up there?"

"Yes, sir."

"So, it seems there were other folks around who may have had an interest in keeping the still a secret?" The defense attorney paced the floor as the prosecutor opened his mouth to begin an objection, but the judge raised a hand to cut him off.

"Please keep to direct questions and answers, Mr. Kimsey," said Judge Wellborn.

"Yes, sir," he replied before turning again to address the witness. "And now about those tracks by the body—how long were they?"

"I don't rightly know."

"And have you ever measured Mr. Justice's foot?"

"No, sir."

"And have you ever measured Mr. Coward's foot?"

"No, sir."

"Can you swear that the tracks by the body belonged to Mr. Justice?"

"No, sir. Can't swear to it."

"What could you tell about what exactly happened there from those tracks?"

"Well, I don't rightly—"

Yes, that's just it; you can't tell. Can you tell which pair of footprints it was who was holding a gun?"

"No, sir."

"Holding a rock?"

"No, sir."

Kimsey stepped toward the jury and faced them, keeping his back to the witness. "So, in summary; you didn't *actually* hear Justice make a threat; you didn't *actually* see him kill someone. You *don't know* that the tracks by the body belonged to Mr. Justice, and there are a number of *other people* who are involved in the still operation that runs around there." He turned on his heel to face the witness. "Is that about right, Mr. Parker?"

"Yes, sir," said Parker with a slightly embarrassed look.

Mr. Kimsey addressed the judge. "Thank you, Your Honor. That will be all."

"Thank you, Mr. Kimsey." Judge Wellborn looked at the prosecutor's table. "Mr. Thompson, redirect?"

"No, sir," said the prosecutor.

"In that case, you may call your next witness," said the judge.

Chapter Thirteen

Tuesday, September 27, 1887

Thompson called for Charlie Rogers, the de-facto leader of the community up by River Mountain, who made his way to the front of the room, was sworn in, and took his seat.

"Mr. Rogers, do you know Tilmon Justice?" asked Thompson.

"Yes, sir."

"How far do you live from him?"

"About a quarter of a mile."

"Did you see him on the morning of the day that James B. Godard was found murdered?"

"Yes."

"About what time?"

"I don't know."

"Where did you see him that morning?"

"He was at my house. He rode up there on his horse."

"What did he come there for?" Thompson crossed over to the table of evidence and leaned forward on it with both hands.

"He came for the gun."

"What kind of gun?"

"A double-barrel shotgun."

"Whose gun is it?"

"Mine."

Thompson pointed to the broken pieces on the table. "Is this the gun he got?"

"Yes."

"What did he say he wanted with it?"

"He said there was some turkeys up in his field eating in his wheat."

"Was he drunk?"

Rogers paused to consider before responding. "Well, he looked like he might have been drinking a little. I expect he wasn't perfectly sober."

"Did you let him have the gun?"

"No. He just come and got it and went off—come in and took it off the rack an' went right back out. Said the turkeys were eating his wheat."

"Is it unusual for someone to just come into your house, take your gun and leave?"

"Not unusual 'tall," said Rogers. "It's the only gun we got up there in the Settlement. If somebody needs it, they can get it an' use it."

"Did he ever bring it back?"

"No."

"When was the next time you saw him?"

"It was later that day, sometime."

"What was Justice's condition then? Was he sober?"

Rogers shrugged slightly. "I don't know. He might have been drinking."

"What time did he come to your house that afternoon?"

"I guess it was between one and two o'clock."

"Did he say anything to you?"

"No, sir. I been down at a little mill that I got down below, an' when I came up to the house, he was there talking to my son-in-law, Osborne Seay. They was there talking, and I just went in."

"What time was it when you heard about Godard's death?"

"About noon, I s'ppose. I was just sitting down to eat dinner when one of Mr. Parker's sons came and told it."

"Then you had heard about it before you saw Justice there that afternoon?"

"I can't recollect, but I s'ppose so."

"What did you do after you heard about the murder?"

"We went down to see the body."

"Can you tell us, did you see any footprints or track around there?"

"I didn't see any plain track. I just saw that the ground was all tore up. Then I came back up to the house and sent some of the boys out for the coroner."

"Mr. Rogers," Thompson turned to face the jury as he posed his next question. "Did you ever have any conversation with Tilmon C. Justice about Old Man Godard?"

"Yes, people tell me all sorts of things. I get asked to make decisions and settle arguments for our folks sometimes," Rogers said with a slight air of pride. He glanced over at the judge with a smile as if to confirm their kindred work, but Judge Wellborn maintained a blank expression. Rogers let it drop and turned back to Mr. Thompson.

"About how long before Godard's death did you talk to Mr. Justice?"

"Might have been a month or so. 'Bout Christmas, certainly."

"What did he tell you then about Godard?"

"Well, nothing 'cept he was a troublesome sort, and in the way."

"Did he make any threats toward him?"

"No sir," said Rogers, with a hint of uncertainty.

"Well, just state what he said about Godard."

"I don't know what all, but Mr. Justice an' him fell out some way about a road or something that Mr. Godard did not want him on and him not passin' through his field."

"Did you hear them talking together about this?"

"No sir, they each talked to me 'bout the other."

"What did you hear Justice say?"

Rogers paused. "Well, now, as for anything that was said specifically, I don't know."

"Give us as much as you can remember about what Justice said about Godard."

He thought for a moment again. "Well, I don't recollect point blank what was said."

Thompson, apparently frustrated by the hemming and hawing, replied tersely. "Well, we haven't got time to wait here; life is too short. Did he say that he was a nice, Christian gentleman?"

"No, sir."

"Did he say he was a rascal and a scoundrel?"

"Well, pretty much."

"Did he say that he ought to be dead?"

Rogers paused, seemingly uncomfortable with the answer he had to give. "Yes, sir."

"Now go on and just tell it. I don't want to pull at you and lead you like I had a corkscrew in my hand."

"Well, I never had anything against either one of them..."

"Just go on and state as nearly as you can what Justice said about Godard."

"Well, I don't know exactly—"

"I didn't ask for exactly,' interrupted Thompson, now clearly irritated. "Where were you whenever you were talking."

"At my house."

"How did the subject come up?"

"Something about the old man talking about his stilling business."

"What did Justice say?"

"Well, I told him about Godard saying that he'd report him, and Tilmon said that if he ever did hunt for his still house, that he'd never hunt another."

"What did you understand that to mean, that 'he'd never hunt another'?"

"Well, I guess he meant that it'd be the last time he ever did such a thing," said Rogers.

"Thank you, that will be all." Thompson returned to his seat, apparently relieved to be done with him.

"Mr. Kimsey, your witness," Judge Wellborn said to the defense attorney, who was already rising from his seat for the cross-examination.

"Mr. Rogers, did you have a house guest that night before the murder?" Kimsey paced the front of the courtroom.

"Yes."

"And who was that?"

"Mr. Jason Coward."

"He stayed all night the night before the murder?"

"Yes, he came to visit his son Silas. Came over from Rabun."

"Was not his son Silas Coward, living with Mr. Justice?"

"I think so."

"What kind of work did Justice have for him to do?"

"I don't rightly know, exactly," replied Rogers evasively.

"Did the old man Coward say anything about that still, or the stilling business, when he was at your house?"

"No, sir.

"When you saw Mr. Justice back at your house later that day, was there anything on him that made you think he'd been out killing anybody?"

"No, sir."

"Did he have blood on him that you could see?"

"No."

"Did he seem upset?"

"No."

"Was he acting any way differently than his usual self?"

"No."

"Do you know whether or not he killed any turkeys?"

"I don't know."

"Mr. Rogers, you didn't see Tilmon Justice kill anyone, and he wasn't covered in blood or anything when you saw him, so how do you know that Mr. Justice was the killer?"

Thompson raised his hand and prepared to offer an objection, but Judge Wellborn rapped his gavel before he could get a word out.

"Mr. Kimsey—no grandstanding! Mr. Rogers is not accusing anyone. Just yes or no questions! Do you understand?"

Rogers was prepared to answer, but he looked perplexed at the conflict going on before and around him and remained silent.

Kimsey turned to Judge Wellborn. "That will be all, Your Honor."

"Thank you, Mr. Rogers," said Welborn. "You may take your seat. Thompson, call your next witness."

The prosecution then called for the testimony of Mr. Jonathan Nicholson. In the gallery, Nicholson's wife nudged him where he sat, apparently lost in his own thoughts, and the sixty-one-year-old man arose and approached the front of the room. The bailiff swore him in before he took his seat in the witness chair.

"Good morning, Mr. Nicholson," said Thompson, continuing immediately and not bothering to wait for a reply. "Can you tell me, Mr. Nicholson, did you know James B. Godard?"

"Yessir."

"Do you know Tilmon C. Justice?"

"Yessir."

"Did you ever have a talk with him about Godard before his death?"

"No, sir." Thompson began to pace the room, turning away from the witness.

"Do you know anything about the relationship between Mr. Justice and Mr. Godard?"

"What was that?" said Nicholson, leaning forward and cupping a hand to his ear.

Thompson repeated the question more loudly and a little more slowly.

"Well, they didn't get along, I reckon," said Nicholson.

"What do you mean by that?" said Thompson, still with the louder voice.

"I think they had a disagreement about a land line or something like that."

"Did you ever see them argue?"

"Well, one time, December, I suppose—that time that Mr. Godard came to church—they had words after, and Tilmon got real mad."

"What words."

"I don' rightly know what they was talkin' about, but Tilmon put his fist in Godard's face, and when I asked him about his shoes I made him, he said he'd stomp him in the mud."

"So, you saw and heard Mr. Justice threaten Mr. Godard, too."

"Well, I don't know so much that he wasn't just sayin' something but not really meanin' it. You see, Tilmon's kinda got a short temper, but I never knowed him to—"

"Yes, we'll get back to that in a minute or so. Were you present the day that Godard's body was found?"

"Yes, I went there with the Parker boys and Mr. Rogers when they came and told it in the Settlement."

"Did you make any search of the area?"

"I looked around to see what he was murdered with."

"And what did you find?"

"We found a rock. And I found some gun locks."

"These?" asked Thompson, pointing to the evidence table.

"I picked up two gun locks, and they's them to the best of my knowledge."

"What about this gun barrel? Do you know whose gun that is?"

"That's the barrel they found buried under the leaves by a log a ways off. I seen that gun several times, and it belongs to Mr. Rogers."

"How was it that Mr. Godard was killed?"

"Looks like that he was shot with shot and then beat with a gun 'til it broke, then beat with that there rock."

"Where were his gunshot wounds?"

"He was shot in the face."

"And then beat?"

"Yes. The whole side of his head was beat in, and every tooth on one side was knocked loose." Some of the ladies in the gallery flinched as Nicholson described the condition of the body.

"With that rock there?" Thompson again pointed to the stained rock on the table.

"Yessir, and the blood and hair was on the rock when we foun' it."

"We've heard Mr. Parker and Mr. Rogers say that there was tracks around the body. Is that true?"

"Yessir. They was in the mud on the day we found him, then froze up solid overnight, so I got a right good look at 'em. They lasted for several days there till the next rain."

"Did you see any tracks leading up to the body?"

"Yes, sir, I saw one track beside Mr. Godard."

"Did you see any other tracks that went near there and stopped?"

"I saw one track a ways off but didn't measure the distance."

"How far do you think?"

"About thirty yards, I'd say."

"Are you sure these tracks were different ones?"

"Yes."

"How do you know."

"Well, the ones around the body was bigger, and the ones a ways off was smaller."

"Were there any other differences?"

"Yes, the bigger ones—the ones around the body—they had tacks in the soles."

"So, two different men, two different sets of shoes, apparently?"

"I think so."

"Where did these tracks go?"

"I saw one track that went near up there to the body, but I didn't measure the distance."

"Well, just how far do you think?"

"About thirty yards."

"Mr. Parker said that there was a smaller set of footprints and a larger set. Was it the large set of tracks that went up to the body or the smaller?"

"The larger ones."

"And the smaller ones, what about them? If they weren't up near the body, where were they?"

"Those tracks didn't follow up the path." They stayed down near the bottom by the branch."

"Mr. Nicholson, please tell the members of the jury and the court here, what is your job? What do you do for a living?"

"Well, I farm some, an' I got a mill an' grind corn an' wheat for folks in the Settlement an' around, but on account of there ain't always work like that to be done, I took to makin' shoes some years back. Pretty good at it, if I do say so. I get supplies when I'm in town, and I can make near about—"

"Yes, thank you, Mr. Nicholson," interrupted Thompson. "I'm sure you're quite good at your trade. Please tell us, how do you affix the soles to the shoe?"

"Well, they's different ways. First, you got to put hot tar or glue on 'em, but then you still gotta fix the edges. For that, you can use an awl an' a hammer an' make punch-holes to sew 'em down, but you can also hammer 'em on."

"Hammer?"

"With small tacks on the sole, while the tar is still soft an' it fixes 'em in."

"Is that common?"

"Mostly see that in store-bought, but I do that some if that's what folks want. Started doin' that in the past couple a years."

"Being the experienced cobbler that you are, you might know about what size shoes made those large tracks that went up to the body?"

"I measured it. It was about a number seven."

"Did you notice anything else about it? What could you tell about the shoes from the prints that it left in the mud?"

"Well, one of the pair of shoes had buck head tacks in the soles, like the ones I use."

"Which one did?"

"The bigger of them had tacks in the soles, and the smaller ones didn't."

"So only one set of tracks went up to the body, and that was the larger set—a size seven—with the tack soles, and they went up the trail to where Mr. Godard was murdered. The smaller set of tracks, the ones with no tacks, they stayed down near the branch. Is that right?"

"Yessir."

"Where did those tracks come from?"

"They came from the direction of Mr. Justice's house. From one of his fields."

"Have you ever seen Tilmon Justice's tracks?"

"Yessir. Frequently."

"Now I will ask you—how did these tracks around the body and Tilmon's compare?"

"Just exactly, according to my judgment. I'd say that the track that was made going to the body was Tilmon Justice's."

Again, the courtroom buzzed with excitement and whisperings. Judge Wellborn pounded his gavel. "Quiet! Quiet in the courtroom!"

"Thank you, Mr. Nicholson." Thompson turned to the judge. "No further questions, Your Honor."

"Mr. Kimsey, you may cross-examine the witness," said Judge Wellborn.

The defense attorney stood and began his line of questioning while adjusting and straightening his jacket. He smiled at the witness but then turned away to face the gallery when he posed his question.

"Mr. Nicholson, can you tell me which unit you were with during the war? Which battles were you involved with?"

Thompson looked at the judge, apparently perplexed. "Your Honor, I object. Is this at all relevant?"

Judge Wellborn raised his hand, silencing the prosecutor. "You may answer the question, Mr. Nicholson."

"What?" said Nicholson.

Judge Wellborn looked at the witness directly this time. "Answer the question."

Kimsey turned to face Nicholson and posed the question again. "What unit were you with in the war? Which battles did you fight in?"

"What was that?" asked Nicholson, leaning forward slightly and putting a hand to his ear.

Kimsey raised his voice slightly. "Who did you fight with in the war?"

Nicholson seemed to get flustered, and his face went pink. "I didn't go off to the war."

"You didn't go fight for Georgia against the Yankees?"

Nicholson paused.

"Mr. Nicholson, did you hear the question?' said Kimsey with a hint of a smirk.

"I went to join up in the militia company, but they let me go after just a month or so."

"And why was that?"

"On account of my hearing ain't good."

Kimsey turned to face the jury. "So, if you don't hear well, I don't think that the jury can trust your account of hearing Mr. Justice allegedly threatening Mr. Godard, as you stated."

"Objection, Your Honor!" Mr. Thompson shot out of his chair.

"I did hear that. I— " Nicholson tried to protest.

Thompson raised his voice to interrupt. "Counsel is way out of line. Not only is this speculative, it's downright argumentative."

"Sustained," said Judge Wellborn as his stare pierced through Kimsey. "You know better. One more like that, and I'll hold you in contempt."

"Yes, Your Honor," said Kimsey, slightly red-faced after the rebuke. He cleared his throat, then addressed Mr. Nicholson again. "So, seeing as you're the local shoemaker, I suppose you know about every pair of shoes for every person in the whole of Towns County?"

Nicholson's irritation rose to the surface. "I didn't say I know ever'body's shoes in the whole county, but I know a good sight of them that live up there with us in the Settlement 'cause I made most of 'em."

"Mr. Nicholson, isn't it true that there are other people who live up at Charlie's Creek who have tacks in their shoe soles?"

"Well, yes, they's some others."

"How many?"

"Just the Parker boys that I know of."

"The boys who found the body that morning, they have tacks in their soles, too?"

"Yes."

"And what day was it that you took the measurements and made the detailed inspection of the tracks? Was it the day of the murder or the next day?"

"The day after, I believe."

"So, it was after all sorts of people were down there to see, and everyone making all sorts of new tracks, and old tracks being stepped on, including other people who have tacks in the soles of their shoes?

"But we all took care to stay— "

Judge Wellborn raised his eyebrows and opened his mouth to speak just as the attorney interrupted the witness. "No need to answer that. I retract the question. Thank you, Mr. Nicholson, that will be all."

The prosecution declined a re-direct examination, and Nicholson returned to his seat in the gallery with his eyes downcast.

Judge Wellborn took out his pocket watch and checked the time. "I think this is a good stopping point for today. We'll resume tomorrow at 9 o'clock." He turned to the jury. "I trust that you will remember the directions that I gave you this morning and that you won't be talking to anybody about today's proceedings—especially any of those newspapermen in the back row." He waved his gavel toward the reporters and then banged it on the table. "Court is adjourned for the day."

Chapter Fourteen

WEDNESDAY, SEPTEMBER 28, 1887

On the second day of the trial, when everyone was back in place and all the initial proceedings were complete, Judge Wellborn nodded to the prosecutor, who then called Elijah Wheeler to come forward. Tilmon's young friend worked his way out of the gallery to the witness stand and was sworn in. He sat down, crossed his arms, and stared defiantly at Mr. Thompson.

Thompson smiled at him with what appeared to be a placating look, perhaps in an attempt to mitigate what was to follow. "Mr. Wheeler, did you know James B. Godard?" he asked.

"Yessir."

"Did you ever have any talk with Tilmon C. Justice about Godard before Godard's death?"

"Nothing in particular," he said, not even slightly masking a tone of disdain.

"Did you ever have any talk that was not particular?"

"No, sir. Not in particular."

The prosecutor crossed his arms, too, and leaned forward slightly. "Mr. Wheeler, did you and Tilmon ever have any kind of talk?" said Thompson, sarcastically.

"Yessir. We have talked," Wheeler shot back.

"When did you ever have any talk with Tilmon Justice about Godard."

"I never had any talk."

"You never talked with him at all?"

"Of course, we talked together."

Exasperated, Thompson continued. "Mr. Wheeler, how long before Godard's death did you talk to Mr. Justice?"

"I can't tell you exactly, 'cause I don't know exactly when Godard died." He smirked and glanced toward the defense table.

The attorney clenched his jaw and took a deep breath. "Okay then, where was it that you talked?"

"I was at Mr. Justice's the morning that Godard was killed."

"Did you talk with him about Godard any that morning?"

"I never heard him say anything about him that I remember. I just went up, and we sat around some, and we just went in and talked like people does."

Thompson placed one hand on the rail of the witness stand and the other in his pocket, leaning in slightly. "About what?"

"I can't rightly recall anything that was said now."

"Did Justice or Coward say anything about Godard that morning?"

"Not that I remember."

"What was Mr. Justice doing?"

"He was sittin' in a chair."

"Did you see him drink anything?"

"I don't remember whether he did or not," he equivocated. "He seemed like he was maybe a little intoxicated."

Thompson slowly walked back to the prosecutor's table and then leaned against it as he faced the witness. "Mr. Wheeler, tell us why you were there that morning and what happened, as best you can recall."

Wheeler replied matter-of-factly. "I just went down there on business to see a man that was owing me a quarter, and while I was sitting there, Mr. Seay came in and told Mr. Justice that the sheep was in his field. Then, Tilmon, he walked out and looked off and come back and picked up a double-barrel shotgun and turned to Mr. Coward and says, 'Come on and let's run out that sheep.'"

"Could you see any sheep in the field?"

"No, sir."

"Did you see anything in his field at all?"

"No, sir."

"How long had you been there when this Mr. Seay came in?"

"Maybe a half hour."

Thompson picked up the gun barrel from the evidence table. "Had you seen the gun before that?"

"No, sir."

"How long was it until you heard the gunshots?"

"I stayed there a little over half an hour after they left. The gunshots came from over in the branch toward where Mr. Godard was killed."

"Where did you go then?"

"I went up to Mr. Nicholson's."

"Did you tell anybody about hearing the gunfire?"

"Not until I heard that the old man was dead. I think it was near to three o'clock."

"When was the next time you saw Mr. Justice?"

"I don't think I saw him until he was arrested."

Thompson put the gun barrel back on the table and relinquished the witness. Kimsey stood to start the cross-examination for the defense. "That gun barrel over there, do you know who loaned it to Mr. Justice?" he asked.

"I first seen it was after it was found. I don't know whose it is," said Wheeler, with a noticeably more agreeable demeanor for the defense attorney.

"Do you know who loaded the gun that morning?"

"No, sir. I don't know whether it was loaded or not."

"Who all went with Justice?"

"Nobody but Jason Coward."

"Did Coward ask you to come with them?"

"No."

"Did Justice say he had a turkey in his field, and that is why he needed the gun?"

"No, sir. Said it was a sheep."

"Did Mr. Justice say that he saw Mr. Godard in his field?"

"He didn't say a word about Godard. He just said sheep."

Kimsey, after a pause, changed to a new line of questioning. "What was Silas doing there at Justice's?"

"I expect he was working there, but I don't know."

"Was Silas working a still there?"

"I don't know, I never seen no still."

"Haven't you heard tell of it?"

"I have heard tell of one being around there, but I never saw it."

Kimsey put his hands behind his back and paced the floor in thought. After one round back and forth, he turned on his heel to face Wheeler. "Didn't you go there to get whiskey?"

"Objection!" barked Thompson once more. "The witness doesn't have to incriminate himself—"

"Sustained. Mr. Kimsey, I warned you..."

"No, I'll answer it," said Wheeler, glowering at the defense attorney. "Like I told you before, Silas had been owing me a quarter, and I went there for that."

"Yes, Your Honor," said Kimsey. He turned to the jury. "So, Mr. Wheeler, on the day of the murder, Justice said he was going to get a sheep out of his field—he didn't say anything about Godard, and furthermore, you didn't see him load the shotgun. Is that right?"

"I 'spect that's 'bout right," he said.

"Thank you, Mr. Wheeler." Kimsey looked at the judge. "That will be all for this witness, Your Honor," he said, taking his seat.

The prosecution declined a redirect examination, and Wellborn gestured to Thompson. "Call your next witness."

Thompson stood. "Your Honor, the prosecution calls Mr. Jason Coward." The elder Coward came forward and took his seat in the witness chair. The bailiff swore him in.

"Do you know Tilmon C. Justice?"

"Yes, sir."

"Did you know James B. Godard?"

"I was just a bit acquainted with him."

"Where did you live on January 17th of this year?"

"I lived in Rabun County."

"How far from Mr. Justice?"

"Some ten or twelve miles."

"Was you well acquainted with Justice?"

"I never did know him until my son went to live over there."

"How many days was it before Godard was killed that you went to Justice's?"

"The day before. I stayed at the Rogers' the night before it happened."

"Where was Justice?"

"At home. My younger son Silas was living with him. I had started out toward my sister's place, and I went by to see him."

"What time did you get to Justice's the morning that Godard was killed?"

"Tolerably soon."

"How long did you stay there?"

Coward shrugged. "'Til about ten or eleven o'clock."

"Where did you go, and who went with you?"

"Mr. Justice left with me. Mr. Seay came by and said that there was a sheep up in his field, and Mr. Justice asked me to go and help him get it out. So I went off with him, and when we got down below the field, he says, 'There's that sheep,' and he cursed and said, 'Come on,' and we went over there and met Mr. Godard. So, Justice says to him, 'Didn't you go and say something?', and then he cocked the gun and then says to me, 'Don't you open your damned mouth, or I'll kill you.' Then he fired the gun and ran a ways up the path to where Godard was and started beating him, and he says, 'Damn you, I guess you won't report anybody else.' Then we went down to where Silas was, and then after a while, we all went on to my sister's."

"Was Mr. Justice drunk or sober?"

"I don't know, I was not too acquainted with him," said Coward.

Thompson looked at the jury and slowly pressed his fist into his other palm four times. "This must have been quite a messy affair, was it not?"

Coward shrugged.

"Where was it that he washed his hand?"

"He washed in a little branch nearby."

"Then what happened?"

"I went an' got Silas, then we went on to my sister's, about six or seven miles on."

"Did you tell anybody that night what had happened?"

"I told my sister and them all about it."

"Thank you, Mr. Coward, that's all." Thompson took his seat as Mr. Kimsey stood and approached the witness stand even before the judge called for him.

"Mr. Coward, so you stayed at Mr. Roger's house the night before the murder, then went down to Justice's in the morning. About what time did you get there?"

"I can't tell you exactly."

"Was it eight or nine o'clock?"

"It was a bit after daylight, but I couldn't tell on account of it being cloudy and rainy some."

"Did you eat breakfast at Justice's?"

"No, I ate at Mr. Rogers'."

"What time was it when you went out to look for the sheep?"

"I don't know, up in the day somewhere, but I couldn't see the sun, so I can't rightly say."

"When you were going to the field with him to get the sheep, where was it that he got the gun?"

"I don't know. I think he got it back about the bed somewhere, but he got it anyway."

"Do you know whose gun that was?"

"He never told me."

"Did you load the gun that morning?

"I did not."

"Was Justice drinking that day?"

"I can't say that I know. He might 'a been."

"You knew he ran a stillhouse up by the branch, didn't you."

"I know there was one, but I don't know what they did there."

"Now, isn't it true that your boy Silas was working at that stillhouse?"

"He was working over here, but I don't know what he was doing."

"Did you go to Justice's to tell him that Godard had reported that stillhouse?"

"No, sir."

Kimsey walked in a circle around the floor of the courtroom, apparently pondering his feet. He stopped and stared straight at the jury, with his back to the witness. "Mr. Coward, weren't you indicted in Rabun County for hog stealing in February of this year?"

"I refuse to answer that," said Coward, indignantly.

Thompson piped up and arose from his chair. "Your honor, this really has nothing to do with the question here. The defense is badgering the witness."

Kimsey turned to the judge. "Your Honor, the character of this witness really has a bearing on the value of this testimony. This information was relevant to decision-making in the first trial."

Wellborn thought for a moment. "You may continue," he said.

Kimsey turned back to face Coward. "At the last court, when I asked you if you were indicted, you said that you did not know."

"On account of I can't neither read nor write." Coward looked to the judge as if for assistance. "I said that I didn't know that I was."

Wellborn interrupted. "If you had been indicted, you would know, wouldn't you?" asked the judge.

"So, were you?" asked Kimsey.

"Yes, sir," said Coward sheepishly.

"Thank you, that will be all, Your Honor," said Kimsey as he returned to his seat with a glance at the prosecutors.

"Redirect?" asked Judge Wellborn.

Thompson shook his head with irritation. "No, Your Honor."

"Then call your next witness," said the judge.

Chapter Fifteen

Wednesday, September 28, 1887

Thompson stood. "Your honor, the prosecution calls Mr. Silas Coward."

Kimsey, suddenly wide-eyed, leaped up. "Your Honor, may we approach the bench?" The judge motioned for them to come forward, and both attorneys leaned over the desk. Kimsey whispered. "They didn't call him as a witness in the first trial!"

"And apparently, we needed some more convincing evidence, didn't we?" said Thompson.

"Your honor, really. It's not right for them to put that boy through this. He's already got trouble enough. It's too much," said Kimsey.

"What do you mean?" asked Judge Wellborn.

"You know, him being deficient and all. Doesn't seem like the right kind of thing to do."

Thompson shook his head and fired back with an urgent whisper. "Your Honor, we're after the whole truth here, and this young man's got a part of it. I don't think it's too much at all. If he's smart enough to run a still, then he's smart enough to testify in court."

Judge Wellborn thought for a moment and looked over the heads of the spectators at Silas, rocking back and forth slightly in the back of the room and fidgeting with his fingers as he awaited their instructions. The judge addressed Kimsey first. "If your man is innocent, then he needs the whole truth, doesn't he?" Then to Thompson, he raised a finger and said firmly, "Don't you be hard on that boy, you hear?" The prosecutor nodded.

The judge waved the young man forward, and he approached the witness seat with his hat clutched tightly in his hands.

"Put your hand on this here Bible," said the bailiff. Silas obeyed. "Do you swear that you will tell the whole truth, and nothing but the truth?" The boy nodded silently and sat down.

"What is your name, son?" asked Thompson.

"Silas Coward. That's a name from the Bible."

"Yes, I see. Were you at Tilmon Justice's house on or about the seventeenth of January this year with your father?"

"Yes, sir."

"What kind of work is it that you do?"

Silas looked at his father, seated in the gallery. The older man shook his head almost imperceptibly and casually put two fingers up to his lips.

"I do what Mr. Justice needs on the farm. Chop wood. Help around there. On account of he only got one arm."

"Did Justice and your father come to where you was working that day?"

"Yes."

"What did Mr. Justice say?"

Silas looked around the room and swallowed. His voice cracked as he replied. "I hardly recollect."

Judge Wellborn spoke. "Just state what you know about the case," he said gently, in an attempt to put the trembling boy at ease.

Silas nodded and then swallowed and looked at the prosecutor. "He said that he'd killed the damnedest big sheep that he'd ever seen."

"Is that all?"

Silas paused. He looked at his shoes, then tilted his head and ran a hand through his hair, smiling to himself.

"Well," prompted Thompson, "is there something else?"

Silas looked up. He chuckled slightly. "He acted like the sheep talked to him."

"What did he say that it said?"

"I don't know. It was sort of funny because... well, I know sheep can't really talk, but Mr. Tilmon, he got down on his knees like he was prayin' and put his hand on his face and said, 'Oh Lord, have mercy on me. Don't kill me, Tilmon.' " Silas recalled the gesture for the courtroom with his hands up to his face. Then peeked through his fingers at the prosecutor before putting his hands down. The courtroom was completely silent.

After a moment, Thompson continued. "What else?"

"Nothin' else, but I thought that was kinda funny. I knew he was just jokin'." Silas looked at the judge earnestly. "Mr. Tilmon, he makes jokes sometimes that don't much seem like a joke unless you know. Like that time he told me he had a hard time playin' the fiddle."

The crowd chuckled, and Judge Wellborn put his hand up to his mouth and looked away for a moment.

"Then what did you do?" asked Thompson.

Silas turned back to the prosecutor. "We stayed there for a little bit, an' then I went over to visit my aunt with my father. She's my daddy's sister. I was kinda sad we didn't go back to Mr. Tilmon's house that night 'cause Miss Annie, she's a good cook, and she pro'lly made some good stew with that sheep."

Thompson turned to Kimsey with a satisfied look and relinquished the witness for cross-examination.

Kimsey stood to address the boy. "How long had you been working with Tilmon Justice?" he asked.

"I had been out there for a month and a half or about that."

"Had your father been to see you?"

"He came that time to see me, the time when Mr. Godard was killed."

"He hadn't been before?"

"No, sir," said Silas, as he wiped his chin and began to fidget.

"Did you ever hear Mr. Godard say anything about that stillhouse?"

"No. I never talked to him at all."

"When your father came to visit, what did he have to say?"

Silas looked uncertain. He glanced at his father who gave him a reassuring nod. "About what?"

"Did your father say anything about Mr. Godard reporting the still?"

"He told me he might would."

"Was that the day that he was killed."

"No, Sir, the day before."

Kimsey, apparently realizing that he couldn't salvage this situation, relinquished the witness and took his seat.

Sensing the tension in the room, Judge Wellborne stood. "This court will recess for lunch a little early today. We'll resume promptly at one o'clock." He rapped his gavel and turned to step down from the dais.

* * *

After the lunch recess, the jury filed back into the room.

"All rise," said the bailiff as Judge Welborn entered. He sat at the bench and rapped the gavel twice on the desk.

"Court's back in session. Mr. Kimsey, the defense may present its case now."

"Your honor, the accused will present his statement, and then I will review our case for the jury during summation."

The manacles on his feet clanked as Tilmon got up from his chair. He shuffled toward the witness stand with the chains scraping behind him on the wooden floor. The bailiff swore him in with his hand on the Bible.

"Mr. Justice, please tell us in your own words what happened on that day," said Mr. Kimsey, barely rising from his seat at the defense table.

Justice looked toward the defense table and kept his eyes fixed on Mr. Kimsey throughout his statement. "Well, Jason Coward come to my house on Sunday evening before this was done on Monday, an' I was not at the house. I was at the stillhouse where his son was, an' he eat his dinner an' came over and told his son about Godard reporting him."

Kimsey stood and interrupted, "Who told what to who?"

"Mr. Jason Coward, he came to my house and told his son, Silas, 'bout that Godard reported about his son and the stillin'.'"

"Go on."

"Then Jason goes up to Mr. Rogers' an' stays all night, and then the next morning he comes down very early and hollers for me an' I gets up an' opens the door an' told him to come in, an' he wanted to know if I had any whiskey."

On the front row behind the prosecutors, Jason Coward shook his head silently and crossed his arms in disagreement.

"Well, we set some out to drink an' commenced to drinking until my wife said we had to go to Galloway's before dinner. Well, I looked up an' saw some sheep up there in my field."

"The field up the hill before you get to Godard's place?" asked Kimsey.

"That's right. Where I got my wheat planted. And I took the gun an' went up there an' saw some turkeys an' shot at one of 'em, an' at the sheep an' they run off. Then I went back to the house, an' Mr. Coward was there. Then Mr. Seay came up directly an' says the sheep is in yer field. An' so I turned to Coward an' ask him if he did not want to go with me, that I had somethin' that I wanted him to look at, an' we went out there and saw Old Godard. Then Coward says to him, 'What did you report about my son for?', and Godard says, 'I didn't do it,' an' he says 'You are a God damned liar,' then he grabbed the gun outta my hand an' cocked it an' shot him or shot at him."

Coward bolted up from his seat in the second row. "Did not! That's a damned lie an' you know it!" The spectators in the room gasped, and conversations started in all corners of the gallery.

"Silence," said Judge Welborn, banging his gavel and then pointing it at Coward. When the room had calmed down, Kimsey nodded for Justice to continue.

"Then he shot again an' then jumped on him an' broke the gun over his head. Then I walked off, an' he come down after me an' I says to him, 'You didn't kill him, did you?', an' he says, 'It'll be a few days before he reports anybody else.' Then we went over an' turned the sheep out an' went down there, and I told him it was time to go to dinner, but he said that he was goin' home. So, I suppose that he went over the mountain. He said before that, I came to him all bloodied up, but I didn't get the gun with the intention of harmin' nobody. I didn't do it."

Kimsey arose from his chair. "Thank you, Mr. Justice. That will be all, Your Honor."

"Mr. Thompson, would you like to cross-examine the accused?" asked the judge.

The prosecutor surveyed the jury for a moment. The men in the jury box watched him watching them. Apparently satisfied with the situation, he stood. "No, Your Honor. I think not."

"In that case, The State may make its summation," said Judge Wellborn.

Tilmon kept his eyes downcast as he made his way back to his seat. Annie sat, weeping silently, in the next row.

Thompson moved from behind the desk and stood before the jury. He paused contemplatively before starting. "Gentlemen, over the past two days, you have heard about the longstanding conflict between Mr. Justice and Mr. Godard, but now you know that Mr. Godard threatened Mr. Justice with notifying the authorities about his illegal activities—and we do understand that it is not the moonshining that is on trial here—but we believe that this became his most compelling motive. We know that Mr. Justice was the last person to have the shotgun, and we know that Mr. Justice had been drinking. Mr. Godard may not have been well-liked, but there was not another person in the Settlement who had such animosity for him as did Mr. Justice. There may have been others that had access to the shotgun, but no one else in the Settlement had a reason to use it in anger against another person except Mr. Justice. I trust that you have no doubts that in his state of intoxication, with the fury in his heart and a gun in his hand, there is no one else in the Settlement who could have killed James Godard," he pounded his hand with his fist three times. "Except. Tilmon. Justice." He looked up and down the jury box and met the eyes of all the men before he continued. "If you've had any doubts over the past two days, then surely Silas's testimony erased them." Thompson covered his face with his hands as Silas had done and peeked through his fingers, scanning the group of stone-faced men in the jury box. Solemnly, he slowly lowered his hands and said, "Gentlemen, you must find him guilty." Thompson returned to his seat.

Judge Wellborn motioned to Kimsey, who stood and began to address the jurors. "There's a lot to take in here, and it may look like the decision is easy," he said, referring to a sheet of notes in his hand, "but consider this. Mr. J. P. Parker only *overheard* a conversation, and he knows that there are others in the area who have an interest in keeping the still a secret. Mr. Rogers saw Tilmon early in the afternoon after the murder. He *wasn't* covered in blood, and he had no signs of being involved in a crime. Mr. Nicholson, the town cobbler, *thinks* that the tracks near the body belong to Mr. Justice. But remember—he said that he also made the boots of the other fellas who tromped all over the scene, and them boots *also* have tacks in the soles. Isn't it possible that the tracks he saw belonged to someone else? Mr. Wheeler saw Tilmon and Coward on the morning of the murder. They weren't angry, and there wasn't no talk of killing Mr. Godard. Most importantly, though, Coward himself was there. He was there in the same place as the victim, he had access to the shotgun, and he had the same motive to keep the still a secret—to protect his son. Tilmon was there too, for sure, but don't you think there's a *doubt* as to who killed Godard?"

Kimsey looked at the lines of silent jurors. "Don't you think there's a doubt?" he said earnestly. "This really just boils down to the word of one man against another, don't it? According to how the law reads, you need to find Justice guilty *beyond a reasonable doubt*. With all that I just said, I don't think you can. There is a doubt. You'll feel that doubt while y'all make your deliberations. That doubt—that's enough to keep a man from hangin'. That doubt is enough to keep a father alive for his children. Gentlemen, there is a doubt, and so you need to find Tilmon Justice not guilty."

Judge Wellborn watched as the defense attorney returned to his seat and gave the forlorn defendant a pat on the shoulder. Annie was seated in the row behind them, stoic and motionless. Kimsey reached back and gave one of her hands a squeeze.

* * *

The jury deliberated for just two hours. As they filed into the courtroom somberly to take their seats, each of the men kept his eyes downcast.

Judge Wellborn rapped his gavel twice. "Gentlemen of the jury, have you reached a verdict?" In the front corner of the jury box, nearest the judge, Hardy Eller stood.

"We have, Your Honor," he said. He gave a folded sheet of paper to the bailiff, who passed it to the judge. Wellborn unfolded it and read it.

"This is your unanimous decision?" asked Wellborn.

"It is."

The judge nodded. Eller took his seat.

"Will the defendant please stand and face the jury?" said Wellborn.

Justice stood and looked around at the courtroom at the faces he knew from the Settlement. The people from the mountain who were at the trial were there not necessarily to support him, and not necessarily to demand justice for Mr. Godard, but as obligated participants in a process they'd rather not have had to endure. Most had a look of resignation, of sadness at what they were about to hear.

They all knew what was coming. Annie sat rigidly in her space on a front bench. A tear ran down her cheek, but her eyes were closed as her lips moved almost imperceptibly in prayer. He looked back at Judge Wellborn, then stared at his now well-worn boots.

"Tilmon C. Justice, the jury finds you guilty of the murder of James Bennett Godard," said the judge. The courtroom gasped. Annie buried her face in her hands and shook with silent sobs. Welborn waited for the shock to subside. He stared at the paper in front of him, and took a deep, fortifying breath before he continued. "Tilmon Justice, now being found guilty, it is my duty to the State of Georgia and to Towns County; I sentence the guilty party to death." With an ever-so-slight shakiness to his voice, he continued. "On November 18th, between the hours of ten o'clock in the forenoon and three o'clock in the afternoon, to be carried to such a place within one-half mile of the town of Hiawassee in said county as may be provided by the ordinary..." Wellborn's voice quivered, and after the next deep breath, he continued. "And that by the said sheriff of said county or his lawful deputy, then and there publicly hanged by the neck until he is dead." Wellborn reached under his robes to fish a handkerchief from his pants pocket and wiped his eyes.

Justice didn't look up, but kept his head bowed as the sheriff's deputies on either side of him turned him around and walked him toward the door. Annie stood, and the men paused for a moment to let Justice put his arm around his wife and their baby. Then the deputies led him back to the jail.

Wellborn struck the gavel on the dais twice as he stood. "Court is dismissed."

Afterword

SACRED TO THE MEMORY OF J. B. GODARD

WAS BORN SEPT. 18 AD 1818

and

DEPARTED THIS LIFE BY BEING MURDERED

JAN. 17 AD 1887

Now here's something interesting! While doing some genealogy research, I found the above epitaph on Find-A-Grave.com attached to my great-great-great grandfather's name. An internet search yielded an online article from the previous March, reporting the apparent theft of that gravestone from its remote site in the Cherokee National Forest, and mentioned a man named Steve Eller as a caretaker for the long-abandoned cemetery, where his ancestors were also buried. I couldn't find any contact information for Steve, so, stabbing blindly, I left telephone messages around in Towns County, Georgia, asking for him to call me. Then I turned to other potential sources of information. The Towns County librarian gave me the number for Sandra Green, the president of the Towns County Historical Society, who, in turn, put me in contact with Mr. Jerry Taylor. He was serving as their vice president and is also the county historian.

If you had to make a list of the most influential citizens of Towns County, Jerry Taylor's name would certainly be included. In addition to teaching history there for thirty-two years, he has served on the school board, plays the organ for several area churches, teaches continuing education classes at Young Harris College, and has been the recipient of numerous civic awards—most recently the 2021 Lake Chatuge Rotary Club's *Citizen of the Year* award.

Jerry Taylor is a living, walking, talking history book. After his first exposure to genealogical records in his youth—transcribing the county census records for his employer—he became well acquainted with all the local names and families. Jerry subsequently served as a census taker for the area himself—in two different decades—and is the county's source of knowledge for all things genealogical. He was instrumental in founding the County Historical Society and the Old Rock Jail Museum in Hiawassee. A graduate of Young Harris College and the University of Georgia, he spent over three decades teaching history at his high school alma mater. Jerry's wife, Beth Banister Taylor, who died in 2005, also taught in the elementary school; and while they had no children of their own, their impact on generations of students and history-minded citizens in Towns County was without dispute.

I called him one afternoon as I was headed home from work.

"Good afternoon Mr. Taylor. Sandra Green referred me to you. My name is Bill Thomas, and I'm the great-great-great-grandson of James Bennett Godard."

There was a distinct pause.

Now that I know Mr. Taylor, I'm sure at that moment, he felt a mixture of surprise and excitement with maybe just a smidge of skepticism.

"Well, you don't say. How do you know that?"

"Well, James Bennett Godard's first wife was Tamsy Caroline Buckalew, and she was my great-great-great grandmother."

"You're right!" he said excitedly. "Not many folks know that."

"Well, I know that. I've heard about him all my life."

"Heard what?"

"Well, how he was a pretty mean guy, and how Tamsy Caroline Buckalew divorced him in the 1840s on the grounds of his "extreme cruelty"—how she had to hide their son, William Thomas Godard, under a bushel basket in the chicken coop to keep him safe whenever her husband came home on a tear. J. B. Godard's first wife, Tamsy Caroline Buckalew Godard Wise, told her granddaughter, Lois, who told her daughter, Effie Belle Thomas Pope, who told it to her sister-in-law, Melba Opal Akins Thomas—who was my own grandmother."

I outlined my Godard ancestry, starting with J. B. Godard's oldest son, William Thomas Godard, and his second wife, Martha Missouri Brown (his first wife and their second child died in 1861); their oldest daughter, Etta Lois Godard, who married David Griffin Thomas; their son David Hugh Thomas who married Melba Opal Akins; and then my father, Judge William Akins Thomas.

We talked for several minutes as I sat in my car. Jerry told me that he had been fascinated by the Godard and Justice events ever since he was a child. He had first heard the story from his own grandmother Rosa Nicholson—who had been taken to see the hanging as a young child and whose point of view is recreated at the beginning of this work. His interest in the events followed him through his teaching career.

In the early '90s, he had one of his high school history classes act out the trial in a self-produced video shot on-scene at the Georgia Mountain Fair Pioneer Village in Hiawassee. He did further research of his own and created a presentation for the historical society about the only hanging that had ever occurred in Towns County—an event which was still occasionally re-told by the oldest residents there, only two or three generations removed from it.

The story of the hanging of the one-armed man is tragic, morbid, and fascinating. Details about Tilmon Justice preaching his own funeral from the gallows with his baby on his knee, and the crowd clamoring for pieces of rope as a souvenir were recounted by Governor Zell Miller in his book *The Miracle of Brasstown Valley*. A man named James Watson caught one of those pieces of rope, which is now in the possession of his great-grandson, William Watson, and the relic has been promised to the Towns County Historical Society, according to Jerry Taylor.

The funeral procession and singing of the hymn "Palms of Victory"—which some boys from Jerry's high school class sang for their video—is documented in the memoir *Happiness from the Blind Side* by John Ferry Moore. The rumor that Justice didn't actually die—but, rather, was quickly cut down and resuscitated—circulated in newspapers nationwide during the months following the hanging but was definitely refuted by Dr. George Hine, one of the attending physicians, in a biting letter to the editor of the *Atlanta Constitution* in February of 1888.

I told Jerry that I wanted to come to visit Towns County, to see Hiawassee, and perhaps to see Godard's gravesite. In November of 2020, he and members of the Towns County Historical Society played host to my wife and me for a memorable visit to the beautiful area in the southern Appalachians and took me up into the mountains to visit the remote cemetery in the Cherokee National Forest. The gravestone hadn't been stolen—that earlier report was erroneous. It seems that the hiker ended up elsewhere and reported on the wrong cemetery.

Jerry gave me a photocopy of the original hand-written court transcript from the book of evidence in the Towns County courthouse and a copy of the video that his students had made in the 1990s. He also authored an article for the local newspaper about our group's outing. Over the course of the next few years, I coordinated with him extensively on the writing of this book, and I am forever grateful for his assistance, encouragement, generosity, and hospitality.

The sensational events around the murder and the trial were reported nationwide in the newspapers of 1887 and 1888, and I have included a number of the articles at the end of this work. I crafted a more focused version of the trial from the court transcript then pieced together the timeline to re-create the personae. In my story, much of the dialogue from the trial is exactly as it was written by the court reporter, Mr. W. S. Richardson, but I have consolidated what was said and amplified what might have happened in the trial for the reader.

I must clarify here for the readers that Jason Coward did not have a son named Silas. Silas is an imagined character that I created to embellish the story. From the actual trial transcript, I combined the testimony of Jason's two sons, David and William, both of whom worked at the still for Tilmon and neither of whom were slow nor afflicted in any way. It is not apparent in the transcript that the town cobbler, Jonathan Nicholson, was hard of hearing. Mr. Taylor provided this detail for me from his own knowledge of the history of the area, and it is included in my dramatization. It is documented in the transcript that the trial hinged on Nicholson's testimony about the sole-tacked prints of the boots that were of his own making and consistent with the ones that he'd made for Tilmon Justice. My transcription of the trial's full handwritten record is posted online, along with the genealogies of Godard, Justice, and Coward, at *www. thefieldofjustice.com.*

Finding more details about James Bennett Godard's life was difficult, even in this age of on-line resources. As I looked for any more information that might have been in our family's possession, my Aunt Sarah Frances Thomas Munzenrider put me in contact with Bill Pope. He is the son of one of her (and my father's) many cousins of that generation, Burnam Pope, who had been the family historian; following his mother Effie Belle Thomas Pope and her aunt Caroline Godard Means in that role. Bill shipped me a big box of old files about William Thomas Godard's children. There was plenty of information that I am sure to use in future projects, but very little information about this estranged patriarch of ours, James Bennett Godard. An unattributed, very old, handwritten note said:

"James Bennett Godard was a farmer and a Justice of the Peace. He lived in Monroe County, Ga. He had also lived in Hiawassee, Ga. Tamsy Caroline Buckalew Godard, his wife, had to leave him because of his great indulgence in whiskey." A notation of Burnam's conversation with my Great-Great-Uncle George Delma Godard, who died in 1960, reported that James Bennett Godard had served in the Georgia State Legislature. A typewritten transcript of a letter from my Great-Great-Aunt Caroline Godard Means included the following: *"My grandfather James Bennett, was murdered in North Georgia. His assailant was hanged at once near the scene of the murder—this man thought that my grandfather reported him for running a 'blind tiger' still. If grandfather did this it was a noble deed, I think."* Additionally, there was a worn cardboard back from a very old book, with no details about what it had been or where it had come from. On aged, water-damaged paper pasted on the inside of the back cover, the words *Back of Vol VIII Gills Com (?)*, are written in a blue ink. Below it there are three names in different ink, all in the same handwriting: *Joseph Godard* and *James B. Godard,* then the third signature begins to follow—*Joseph Godard*, again before it appears that the pen runs out. This artifact remains a complete mystery.

Thanks to the additional research by Jerry Taylor and the Deputy Towns County Historian, Mr. Jason Lee Edwards, we have been able to piece together pretty certain milestones in the life of my great-great-great grandfather. In the oldest document that we know of, James Godard is listed in the 1840 census in Pike County, Georgia, with a wife under age 20 and a male child under five. This would be Tamsy Caroline Buckalew Godard and William Thomas Godard, since Pike and Lamar Counties are the historical home place for the Thomas, Godard, and Akins families. We can find no documentation of James and Tamsy's divorce, but our family story is that the divorce was granted on the grounds of "extreme cruelty", and the story of hiding the children from a drunken father is also part of the narrative. The divorce must have been about 1842 after the other two children were born. Divorce would have been quite unusual, and an interesting wrinkle serves as a notorious testament to the character of James Bennet Godard (JBG), as apparently, the court also ordered that he not be permitted to marry again. We think this was the case, because in 1853 there was a bill introduced in the Georgia Legislature by Mr. E. M. Reid of Carroll County for the relief of this injunction. The matter passed in the house, but not in the senate.

JBG married again, anyway. In March of 1847, a DeKalb County, Georgia marriage was documented between James B. Goddard (spelled thus) and Jane Harris. Later, in the 1850 Census in Carroll County, we find *Jas. B Goddard* (age 32 and born in Georgia, so the age fits) and Jane (age 31, born in North Carolina) enumerated with five children between ages 4 and 14. His occupation was listed as grocer. The relationships are unclear, and it's likely they were all her children from a previous marriage, though the youngest children may have been fathered by JBG. Property records show that JBG purchased parcels of land in Carroll County in 1850 and 1852 and sold one for taxes in 1855. The available court records for Carroll County only begin in 1857, so it is unclear where, when, or if JBG and Jane Harris Godard divorced.

Fannin County, Georgia, was created from the western portion of Union County in 1854. JBG's father, Joseph Godard of Spalding County, Georgia, sold him some land in Fannin County in 1854, and it was in Fannin County that JBG was admitted to the bar in 1856. There is no record of Jane Godard, but apparently JBG took up with a Miss Elizabeth Paxton, known as 'Babe' or the 'buttermilk whore', and they lived together. The court charged JBG with living in adultery and a state of fornication in November of 1856, and he was subsequently found guilty and required to pay a $50 fine—but the couple fled, apparently without paying. We know this because of the advertisement that the Fannin County Sheriff placed in a newspaper.

* * *

19 February 1857

The Cassville Standard, (Cassville, Georgia)

Twenty-five Dollars Reward.

The above reward will be paid for the delivery of
James B. Godard and Elizabeth Paxton who lately
runaway from Fannin County.
T. R. Trammell, Sheriff

* * *

It seems that JBG and Babe Paxton moved to Towns County (created from the eastern portion of Union County in 1856), where he was involved in the altercation with William R. McConnell. JBG stabbed him with a knife, and the next day he was beaten severely in retribution. It was Judge Wellborn on the bench in Towns County then who threw out the case and called it even. James B. Goddard (spelled thus) is documented in the 1860 census in Hiawassee, where he is listed as a 41-year-old attorney-at-law with Elizabeth, aged 30. We think this was Elizabeth 'Babe' Paxton, not Eveline Elizabeth Sweat.

Civil war records have James Godard as a private assigned to the hospital in Augusta and possibly at the hospital in Griffin. It seems unusual that he would be assigned as a corpsman, since a literate man in his fourth decade, with training as an attorney, could easily have been given a different role in the Confederate forces. After the war, Godard took the amnesty oath in Towns County, on 23 August 1865, where Martin Burch, the Towns County Ordinary, provided us with a physical description: "dark complexion, dark hair, gray eyes, 47 years old and by profession a lawyer, is five feet 4 inches tall." JBG is listed in the *Returns of Qualified Voters and Reconstruction*

Oath Book in August of 1867, where he stated that he resided in the election precinct 990 of Towns County. His signature there looks like the one in the book cover artifact that I have.

The marriage of JBG and Eveline Elizabeth Sweat (b. ~ 1837) was documented on 8 September 1873 in Walton, Georgia. JBG is listed in two of the tax digests of Towns County (1871-1875), but only one entry has Elizabeth E. Godard listed with him—where she is documented to have property worth $75 in the city, and he is listed as a voter. In 1882 JBG and Eveline would move to the mountains, where in just over five years' time, Old Man Godard would meet his demise. The Towns County deed book documents their purchase of the land up in the far northeast corner of the county.

* * *

13 January 1882,

Samuel N. Owen to James B. Godard and Eveline E. Godard,

> *$150, 100 acres of LL 74 and LL 87, beginning at the original line at or near Charley's Creek thence east with the corn line to the top of the river mountain then still a east course with a marked line to a Spanish oak marked and agreed on by the parties thence North west course to the conditional line thence a west course to the original in the north west corner thence a south course to the beginning.*

* * *

Other than the report about the runaways from Fannin County and the stories of his murder, there doesn't seem to be much more news about our man in Georgia's historical newspapers. Some other entries that I did find may clear up one point of my family's oral history that has been confusing, namely that JBG had served in the state legislature. A slave owner named James Godard, from Jones County in 1830, was a Whig party state senator for the 25th district

(Jones and Putnam Counties) and served in that role into the 1840s. That man had been the agent and executor for the estate of a man, apparently a relative, named Joel Godard. There is, however, no Joel Godard to be found in our family tree, and our JBG was only 12 years old in 1830, so likely, this is a different James Godard. Nevertheless, the name certainly could have caused the descendants in my grandparents' generation—none of which our JBG ever knew— to make some assumptions about service in the legislature. I'm not sure about any of this at all—but it leaves much to be imagined!

After much searching, Jerry Taylor found Tamsy Caroline Buckalew Godard in the 1850 census in Monroe County, Georgia. The misspelled transcriptions of the handwritten last names from the census document (Gardner instead of Godard, and Buckner instead of Buckalew) are what created the confusion. The document shows her there with William (age 12) and Joseph (age 9 and noted as 'idiotic'—he died young), living next door to her father William with his second wife and four children. It is curious that Anna (who would have been about 8 then) is not documented. Tamsy didn't marry again for many years. She and her second husband, Witt C. Wise (1810-1877) married in 1870, and they lived together in Pike County, Georgia. Witt was apparently highly esteemed in the family, as Tamsy's daughter Anna named her own son after him. Tamsy died of breast cancer on her 66th birthday in 1877, just ten months after JBG was murdered. She is buried in Lamar County, Georgia at the Liberty Hill Primitive Baptist Church cemetery, and her original gravestone was supplemented with a second one in later years by some of her descendants.

Tamsy Caroline Buckalew Godard – Wise

October 22 1821 - October 22 1887

Grand-Daughter of Frederick Buckalew

Revolutionary Soldier

GODARD GENEALOGY

Three Generations of Descendants of

James Bennett Godard (1818-1887) and
Tamsy Caroline Buckalew (1820-1887)

(Compiled from Various Sources)

1. William Thomas Godard (WTG) (1838 - 1908)
    m. Isabella Loviey Hardin (ILH) (1838 - 1861)
    m. Martha Missouri Brown (MMB) (1846 - 1927)

    (of WTG and ILH)

    1.1. Thomas Thella Godard (1860 - 1877)

    1.2. Mary Eugenia Godard (1861 - 1861)

    (of WTG and MMB)

    1.3. Rev. George Delma Godard (1869 - 1960)
    m. Elizabeth Alice Williams (1874 - 1950)

    1.3.1. William Wallace Godard (1898 - 1980)

    1.3.2. Mary Elizabeth Godard (1905 - 1971)

    1.4. Etta Lois Godard (1872 - 1940)
    m. David Griffin Thomas (1870 - 1928)

    1.4.1. Effie Belle Thomas (1896 - 1987)

    1.4.2. William Addison Thomas (1889 - 1962)

    1.4.3. Douglas Fain Thomas (1900 - 1963)

    1.4.4. David Hugh Thomas (1901 - 1945)

    1.4.5. (Twin) George Delma Thomas (1901 - 1901)

1.4.6. Burnam Daniel Thomas (1901 - 1920)

1.4.7. Martha Virginia Thomas (1906 - 1986)

1.4.8. Caroline Elizabeth Thomas (1909 - 1991)

1.4.9. James Howard Candler Thomas (1911 - 1997)

1.4.10. Frances Thomas (1914 - 2001)

1.5. Anna Belle Godard (1874 - 1921)
    m. Dr. Young Rufus Coleman (1870 - 1953)

1.5.1. Thomas Virgil Coleman (1899 - 1954)

1.5.2. Roy Godard Coleman (1902 -1926)

1.5.3. John Rufus Coleman (1914 - 1980)

1.6. Dr. Robert Fain Godard (1876 - 1940)
    m. Susie Davis (1886 - 1971)

1.6.1. Robert Fain Godard (1908 - 1910)

1.6.2. Jefferson Davis Godard (1912 - 1940)

1.6.3. Martha Godard (1915 - 1995)

1.6.4. Sarah Etheridge Godard (1920 - 1991)

1.7. Caroline Godard (1879 - 1962)
    m. James Clarence Means (1878 - 1961)

1.7.1. James Clarence Means Jr. (1912 - 1991)

1.7.2. Herman Fain Godard Means (1914 - 1970)

1.8. Dr. William Burnam Godard (1881 - 1935)

1.9. Minnie Armasia Godard (1884 - 1884)

2. Joseph Godard (1840 - 1846)

3. Anna Elizabeth Godard (1842 - 1917)
    m. Robert B. Cowell (1834 - 1909)
    (This name is variably reported in records as Colwell or Caldwell)

3.1. Emma Willie Caldwell (1864 - 1932)
    m. Isaac Lafayette Lazenby (1856 - 1932)

3.1.1. Robert Lafayette Lazenby (1881 - 1881)

3.1.2. Eddie Lazenby (1882 - 1882)

3.1.3. Thomas Judson Lazenby (1883 - 1964)

3.1.4. Anna Ethel Lazenby (1885 - 1955)

3.1.5. John Henry Lazenby (1887 - 1887)

3.1.6. Mamie Bell Lazenby (1888 - 1966)

3.1.7. Emmet G. Lazenby (1891 - 1908)

3.1.8. Willie Odessa Lazenby (1893 - 1966)

3.1.9. Roy Duffie Lazenby (1899 - 1899)

3.1.10. Troy Bonds Lazenby (1899 - 1950)

3.1.11. Cullen Lazenby (1901 - 1901)

3.2. Dr. Joseph Glenn Colwell (1865 - 1924)
m. Annie Lee Edwards (1869 - 1944)

3.3. Robert Lee Colwell (1868 - 1910)
m. Lillian Lee Norris (1872 - 1958)

3.3.1. William Homer Caldwell (1891 - 1957)

3.3.2. Eulice Caldwell (1892 - 1973)

3.3.3. Ethel Caldwell (1894 - 1973)

3.3.4. Annie Caldwell (1896 - 1957)

3.3.5. Dewey Caldwell (1898 - 1958)

3.3.6. Katie Lee Caldwell (1901 - 1986)

3.4. Harriett C. Colwell (1870 - 1923)
m. William Lee Akins (1869 - 1963)

3.4.1. William Glenn Akins (1889 - 1949)

3.4.2. Ella Ruth Akins (1893 - 1981)

3.4.3. O'Kelly Wright Akins (1895 - 1966)

3.4.4. Joseph Virgil Akins (1906 - 1954)

3.5. Witt C. Wise Colwell (1872 - 1928)
m. Minnie Louisa Dearing (1874 - 1946)

3.5.1. Corine Elizabeth Colwell (1893 - 1941)

3.5.2. Mattie Mae Caldwell (1896 - 1981)

3.5.3. George Spencer Caldwell (1897 - 1946)

3.5.4. Annie Katie Caldwell (1898 - 1916)

3.5.5. John Robert Caldwell (1902 - 1962)

3.5.6. Minnie Leona Caldwell (1904 - 1982)

3.5.7. Vera Lois Caldwell (1905 - 1982)

3.5.8. Joseph Clifford Caldwell (1906 - 1982)

3.5.9. Rosa Pinke Caldwell (1909 - 1992)

3.5.10. Florrie Jean Caldwell (1910 - 1973)

3.5.11. Laura Caldwell (1912 - 1986)

3.5.12. Julia Witt Caldwell (1913 - 1991)

3.5.13. Mabelle Wise Caldwell (1917 - 1986)

3.6. William Henry Farmer Colwell (1873 - 1926)
    m. Ida Lucinda Burnett (1875 - 1917)

3.6.1. Martha Elizabeth Caldwell (1894 - 1894)

3.6.2. William Lewis Colwell (1896 - 1980)

3.6.3. Alma Bell Colwell (1898 - 1909)

3.6.4. Alfred Lewis Colwell (1899 - 1978)

3.6.5. Joshua Dikes Colwell (1899 - 1978)

3.6.6. Robert Burnett Colwell (1901 - 1924)

3.6.7. Eddie Roy Colwell (1903 - 1991)

3.6.8. Raymond Colwell (1905 - 1989)

3.6.9. Joel Thomas Colwell (1907 - 1973)

3.6.10. James Alton Colwell (1909 - 1909)

3.6.11. Rosa Mae Colwell (1910 - 1991)

3.6.12. Henry Clarence Colwell (1914 - 1935)

3.6.13. Bertha Louise Caldwell (1915 - 1916)

3.7. Thomas Barnes Colwell (1876 - 1959)
m. Lillie Belle Marable (1884 - 1969)

    3.7.1.   Jesse George Colwell (1899 - 1984)

3.8. Eunice Ethel Colwell (1878 - 1964)
m. John William Spruce (1873 - 1956)

    3.8.1.   Daniel Robert. Spruce (1872 - 1979)

    3.8.2.   Thurman Parker Spruce (1904 - 1983)

    3.8.3.   Wesley Camp Spruce (1907 - 1984)

    3.8.4.   Cisby F. Spruce (1910 - before 1920)

    3.8.5.   Camille Spruce (1919 - 2000)

3.9. Rosa Ann Colwell (1882 - 1952)
m. Frank Brown Coulon (1880 - 1956)

    3.9.1.   James Corry Coulon (1903 - 1954)

    3.9.2.   Myrtie Frances Coulon (1904 - 1991)

    3.9.3.   Elsie Elizabeth Coulon (1908 - 1996)

    3.9.4.   Frank Brown Coulon Jr. (1910 - 1973)

    3.9.5.   Rosa Ann Coulon (1914 - ?)

3.10. Tillman Oxford Colwell (1886 - 1944)
m. Nina Stallings (1902 - 1934)

    3.10.1. Jack Caldwell (1923 - 2009)

    3.10.2. Clarice Clare Caldwell (1924 - 2000)

    3.10.3. Tilman Oxford Caldwell Jr. (1925 - 2002)

    3.10.4. Pearle Ray Caldwell (1928 - 2010)

JUSTICE GENEALOGY

Three Generations of Descendants of

Tilmon C. Justice (1857 - 1887) and
Georgia Ann Darnell (1862 - 1930)

(Compiled From Various Sources)

1. Isaac Benson Justice (1879 - 1962)

   m. Isabell York (1881 - 1918) had 3 children

   m. Mary McDowell (1908 - 1998) had 8 children

     1.1. Benson Broughten Justus (1910 - 1952)
       m. Olive Sanders (1908 - 1992)
         1.1.1. Peggy Ann Justus (1934 - ?)
           m. John Thomas Winters (1929 - 1990)
         1.1.2. Jonathon B. Justus (1937 - 2005)

     1.2. Anna Juanita Justus (1912-1991) (buried in Macon County, NC)
       m. William Hopper (1912 - 1991)

     1.3. Launnah Justice (1916 - 2006)
       m. Arthur Thomas Cline, Jr. (1917 - 2000)
         1.3.1. Arthur Thomas Cline, III (1948 - ?)
         1.3.2. Linda Cline (1951 - ?)

     1.4. Hattie Juanita Justus (1920 - 2011)
       m. William Hopper (1921-1997)(buried in Habersham County, GA)
         1.4.1. William Jack Hopper (1943 - 1992)

        1.4.2. Robert B. Hopper (1947 - 1965)

        1.4.3. Dianna M. Hopper (1948 - 2014)

        1.4.4. Dorothy Sue Hopper (1950 - 2013)

1.5. Savannah Justice (1924 - 2014)

    m. Buster Brown Welborn (1918 - 1985)

        1.5.1. Alton Nelson Welborn (1939 - 2015)

1.6. Allyn Justus (F) (1925 - ?)

1.7. Fannie Mae Justice (1928 - 2007)

    m. Nova Stephens (1911 - 1976)

1.8. Tilmon C. Justice (1929 - 1993)

    m. Frances Louise Welch (1935 - 2007)

1.9. Virginia Iola Justice (1932 - 2016)

    m. Almon Jiles (1876 - 1964) (had two children)

    m. Frank Sexto (1924 - 1983)

    m. Henry Edward Ivester (1932 - 2019)

        1.9.1. Fred Duncan Jiles (1952 - ?)

        1.9.2. Patricia L Jiles (1962 - 2017)

1.10. Ibby Justice (1934 - 2005)

    m. William Hoyt Bradley (1936 - 2009)

1.11. James R. Justice (1940 - ?)

2. Lura Viola Justice (1885 - 1944)

m. John E. Crawford (1864 - 1926) (he had children by his prior marriage)

3. Luther Grenville Justice (1887 - 1954)

    m. Lillie Effie Leathers (1899 - 1970)

    3.1. Luther Carl Justice (1916 - 1993)

        m. Lorena Daniel (1917 - 2006)

    3.2. Jack Warren Justice (1919 - 1993)

        m. Virginia Fagan (1922 - 2012)

COWARD GENEALOGY

Two Generations of Descendants of

Jason Coward (1835 - 1905) and
Artemissa Chastain (1837 - 1903)

(Compiled From Various Sources)

1. Julius M. Coward (1855 – 1863)

2. Edward J. C. Coward (1857 - 1859)

3. Sarah Emmaline "Sallie" Coward (1859 - 1905)
   m. Jesse C. Wood (1853 - 1943)
   3.1. Lewis Wood (1879 - 1953)
         m. Catharine Jones (1883 - 1965)
   3.2. Viola Mae Wood (1885 - 1915)
         m. General Garfield Meeks (1883 - 1957)

4. William Jason Coward (1862 - 1934)
   m. Maryann Elizabeth Meeks (1864 - 1959)
   4.1. Nancy L. Cowart (1886 - 1906)
         m. Charles Joseph Williams (1881 - 1939)
   4.2. David Alonzo Cowart (1888 - 1967)
         m. Lemma Odell Bradford (1897 - 1974)
   4.3. Zora Pearlie Cowart (1891 - 1974)
         m. Charles Joseph Williams (1881 - 1939)

4.4. Mary Gertrude Cowart (1896 - 1919)

    m. George Jackson Towler (1890 - 1967)

5. Thomas David Coward (1864 - 1936)
m. Nancy Arminda Powell (1867 - 1927)

    5.1. Nancy Elizabeth Coward (1887 - 1983)

        m. Willie H. Johnson (1884 - 1924)

    5.2. Vassie Artemissia Coward (1891 - 1985)

        m. Ernest Cleo Dogen (1893 - 1959)

    5.3. Bessie Coward (1894 - 1994)

        m. William B. Walraven (1897 - 1969)

    5.4. Cora Ann Coward (1896 - 1993)

        m. Thomas Milton Hartsfield (1891 - 1962)

    5.5. Millie Coward (1900 - 1976)

        m. Alver Jay Dison (1897 - 1974)

    5.6. Stella M. Coward (1889 - 1963)

        m. Dan Coward (1900 - 1976)

    5.7. Sarah Coward (1900 - ?)

        m. ? Haney (?-?)

    5.8. Effie Mae Coward (1902 - 2002)

        m. Ralph Woodward (1898 - 1964)

    5.9. Clara Coward (1903 - 1987)

        m. Walter Washington Taylor (1905 - 1941)

    5.10. David Dewey Coward (1905 - 1980)

        m. Charlotte Camp (1915 - 1997)

    5.11. John Powell Coward (1907 - 1987)

        m. Sallie Maude Westmoreland (1911 - 2001)

6. Ruthie Ann Texas Coward (1867 - 1946)
m. James Meredith Moreland (1862 - 1948)

6.1. Ira R. Moreland (1888 - 1955)

    m. Myrtle Ophelia Johnson (1886 - 1960)

6.2. Lona Arizona Moreland (1888 - 1985)

    m. Charles Andrew Shook (1886 - 1966)

6.3. Lorrie Moreland (1889 - 1937)

6.4. Mattie Moreland (1892 - 1929)

    m. John Wm. Oscar Hamilton (1880 - 1963)

6.5. Lassie Moreland (1893 - 1950)

    m. William Grant Deaver (1884 - 1967)

6.6. William Sylvester 'Veck' Moreland (1895 - 1974)

    m. Althea Bradshaw (1893 - 1990)

6.7. Dean Ireland Moreland (1889 - 1985)

    m. Dora Belle Dayton (1906 - 2001)

6.8. Vassie Vandora Moreland (1902 - 1996)

    m. John Leonard Eller (1902 - 1973)

6.9. Ice Mae Moreland (1906 - 1993)

    m. Caney Lee Rogers (1898 - 1992)

7. Adinah Missouri Coward (1869 - 1945)
m. Charles Nichols (1862 - 1916)

7.1. Lillie Nichols (1886 - ?)

    m. J. B. Frady (1886 - ?)

7.2. Claud Ernest Cowart (1887 - 1967)

    m. Jean Lou Dessler Parr (1884 - 1967)

7.3. Zora Teresa Belle Nichols (1890 - 1971)

    m. Samuel J Waters (1882 - 1960)

7.4. Paris Greenville Nichols (1892 - 1959)

    m. Polona Margaret Bradshaw (1895 - 1989)

7.5. Ethel Effie Nichols (1894 - 1987)

    m. Lawrence Carden Nicholson (1890 - 1959)

7.6. William Virgil Nichols (1898 - 1978)

    m. Vicie Mae Clark (1906 - 1945)

7.7. Charles Glenn Nichols (1902 - 1976)

    m. Gladys Medisto Kilby (1903 - 1989)

7.8. Inez Myrtle Nichols (1905 - 1991)

    m. Cuba Nelson Bradshaw (1882 - 1970)

7.9. Lela Missouri Nichols (1907 - 2000)

    m. Estelle Esco Nichols (M) (1905 - 1989)

7.10. Norma C. Nichols (1909 - 1988)

    m. Thomas Lester Clark (1904 - 1974)

8. Talitha Izora Coward (1872 - 1939)
   m. John G. Moreland (1872 - 1940)

    8.1. Winford Grady Moreland (1897 - 1959)

    8.2. Garnett J. Moreland (1899 - 1971)

        m. Annie Cornelia Barnett (1896 - 1971)

    8.3. Maudie Moreland (1902 - 1922)

    8.4. Ervin Jason Moreland (1903 - 1967)

        m. Rose Ethel Heath (1906 - 1999)

    8.5. Minnie Annabelle Moreland (1905 - 1976)

        m. Richard William Barnett (1882 - 1953)

    8.6. Henry Moreland (1906 - 1906)

    8.7. Victor Paul Moreland (1914 - 1969)

        m. Esther Herndon (1910 - 2001)

9. Taylor Venaldo Coward (1873 - 1930)
   m. Callie Missouri Meeks (1876 - 1945)

9.1. William Cowart (1899 - 1973)

    m. Mary Levenia Smith (1904 - 1976)

9.2. Annie Liza Cowart (1900 - 1959)

    m. Carl Cowart (1908 - ?)

9.3. Earnest G. Cowart (1900 - 1975)

    m. Annie Rosie Lee Smith (1900 - 1972)

9.4. Verlee Cowart (1908 - 1998)

    m. Milton Alfred McConnell (1904 - 1994)

9.5. Elizabeth M. Cowart (1911 - ?)

9.6. Leroy Lincoln Cowart (1911 - 1994)

    m. Mary Agnes Smith (1913 - 1995)

9.7. Troy Chambers Cowart (1914 - 1982)

    m. Cora Jane Alewine (1923 - 2005)

9.8. Benjamin Cowart (1916 - 1992)

    m. Francine Smallwood (1917 - 1999)

10. L. Maggie Coward (1876 - 1903)
m. Patrick Littleton Meeks (1871 - ?)

10.1. James H. Lester Meeks (1896 - 1965)

10.2. Lillie L. Meeks (1898 - 1983)

    m. Lester Dalton (1900 - 1959)

10.3. Lena Meeks (1899 - 1906)

10.4. Lula Bertie Meeks (1902 - 1978)

    m. Ben H. Stone (1902 - 1985)

10.5. Margie Meeks (1906 - 1914)

11. Mary L. Coward (1880 - 1943)
m. Joel Washington Phillips (1877 - 1943)

11.1. Flora Hassie Phillips (1897 - 1933)

    m. William Franklin Gilbert (1891 - 1942)

11.2. Lawrence Phillips (1900 - ?)

11.3. Paralee Leola Phillips (1903 - 1995)

    m. Lish Washington Ledford (1901 -1976)

11.4. Luola Phillips (1905 - 1962)

    m. Richard Benjamin Moss (1899 - 1991)

12. Joseph Lester Coward (1880 - 1943)
m. Connilee Gilbert (1884 - 1964)

12.1. Verna May Cowart (1902 - 1990)

    m. Henry Grady White (1890 - 1969)

12.2. William Caney Cowart (1904 - 1994)

12.3. Joseph Claude Cowart (1905 - 1985)

    m. Losa Hestina Shook (1903 - 1975)

12.4. Franklin Clyde Cowart (1908 - 1980)

    m. Christine Flanagan (1916 - 2009)

12.5. Barnet Clinton Cowart (1911 - 1974)

    m. Onie Lou Patterson (1915 - 2000)

12.6. Edna Sally Cowart (1913 - 1949)

    m. John Pete Flanagan (1914 - 1949)

12.7. Nola Cleo Cowart (1916 - 1939)

    m. John Gurley Gibson (1913 - 1991)

12.8. Leona Elizabeth Cowart (1919 - 2007)

    m. William Pruitt (1919 - 1982)

12.9. Clara Connilee Cowart (1922 -1993)

    m. Dolly Jefferson Trusty (1918 - 1981)

12.10. Thomas Grady Cowart (1925 - 2000)

    m. Alva Agnes Nichols (1931 - 2002)

12.11. Lillie Viola Cowart (1929 - 1981)

    m. James Harrison Bright (1930 - 1982)

Newspaper Reports

23 January 1887

Atlanta Constitution (Atlanta, Georgia)

SHOT DEAD
THE TERRIBLE CRIME OF AN ILLICIT DISTILLER

He Shoots an Old Man Down Because He Feared Exposure—
The Body Robbed of Five Dollars—Another Murder in Dawson
County—People Greatly Excited, Etc.

CLARKESVILLE, Ga., January 22.—[Special.] T. C. Justice, of Towns county, was lodged in jail at this place by Sheriff Harlden, under charge of murdering J. B. Goddard. The sheriff's statements are as follows, taken from the evidence before the coroner's jury:

J. C. Coward testified that there are two fields belonging to Justice. Justice saw Goddard crossing one of them. He said to Coward:

"Go with me to the sheep ranch."

So he took down his gun and started, but instead of going there, he went in below where Goddard was crossing, and on his way he said:

"See the old fellow looking round. I think he had better wear glasses before he looks for my still, but I will make him look through a double gun."

THE FATAL SHOT.

Coward did not think about his intentions, so he stopped Goddard and says: "I will kill you." Goddard begged for mercy, and Coward begged for him, but still Justice shot him twice, in the head and arm. Not satisfied with that, he beat his head badly with his gun, till it was broken. He then used a rock for some time, breaking the left arm and skull. Coward was not allowed to interfere for fear of Justice, who threatened him, and afterwards told him if he ever revealed his act he would kill him. Justice was covered with blood when he returned, and before reaching his home hid the broken gun one hundred yards from where the murder took place. Fifteen witnesses testify that he had threatened Goddard for an old grudge and for fear he would report him for stilling. The killing took place about twelve o'clock in the day, and the body was discovered by J. P. and David Parker, fifteen miles from Hiawassee, on the Tallulah river. The arrest was made before a warrant was issued, and as soon as one could be obtained and the jury summoned a regular trial was held. J. P. Burrong represented the state, and W. I. Blackwell the prisoner.

GUILTY OF MURDER

A verdict was found for premeditated murder. Goddard was seventy years of age and had no family but his wife. He was a man in good standing. Justice has a wife and three children, and is classed as a stiller. He is a man of good sense. He has one arm and with that exception is a man of powerful strength. Mrs. Goddard claims that her husband had on his person five dollars and forty-five cents in money, which was gone when they found him.

The prisoner, on being interviewed denied the charge and says he had threatened to kill Goddard if he reported him and that was as far as he acknowledged.

24 January 1887

The New York Times (New York, New York)

MURDER BY A MOONSHINER.
HE SHOOTS AN OLD MAN AND
NARROWLY ESCAPED LYNCHING

CLARKESVILLE, Ga, Jan. 23.—Towns County came near having a lynching when the murderer of Mr. J. B. Goddard was discovered to be J. C. Justice, living near Hiawassee. When the body of Goddard was discovered in the cornfield of Justice it was riddled with shot, and the flesh was hacked in a shocking manner, evidently by a piece of stone which was found nearby. The neighborhood was wrought into a high state of excitement. The mysterious disappearance of Justice directed suspicion toward him, which materialized when J. C. Coward admitted that he had been a witness of the murder, and that Justice was the murderer. Justice had been for years an illicit distiller and was looked upon as a leader among the moonshiners. Of late several raids have been made around the neighborhood by the officials. Justice insisted that Goddard was furnishing information to the Government, and said there would be no peace until he was put out of the way. Several days ago, while Coward was on a visit to Justice, they saw Goddard going across the cornfield. "He is after my sheep ranch," said Justice. This is the name which the distillers have for their retreats. "I think he had better wear glasses before he looks for my still, but I will make him look through a double gun." Saying this, Justice got his double-barreled shotgun and, quietly crossing the field, met Goddard. He put the muzzle to the old man's head and fired. A second shot penetrated the lungs. As his victim fell wounded to death Justice belabored him with his gun until he broke the stock. He then began the mutilation of the body with a sharp stone, when Coward ran up and attempted to stop him. The enraged man, covered with this victim's blood, turned upon Coward and threatened to kill him if he ever "peached" on him. The officers found the murderer at the house of a neighbor where he had secreted himself, still wearing his bloody clothes. He was hurried off to jail at Clarksville, where he now is. Goddard was 70 years of age and in good circumstances. Justice is about 35, with a wife and five children. The illicit distillers generally sympathize with Justice but the better class of people were so outraged that they would have made short work of him if they had caught him.

12 February 1887

Savannah Morning News (Savannah, Georgia)

Near Clayton Wednesday night Sheriff W. T. York and posse succeeded in capturing the notorious Jason Coward and his two sons, Thomas and David. Coward and his sons are under bond of $300 for their appearance at the March term of Rabun Superior Court to answer to the charge of simple larceny. The old man is implicated as an accessory to the murder of old man Goddard by Tilman Justin. (sic) It was reported that the revenue officials are after him for moonshining. The securities on the bond became uneasy, hence the capture and delivery.

23 February 1887

Atlanta Constitution (Atlanta, Georgia)

THREE MURDERERS
WHO LOCK UP THE JAILER AND ESCAPE

A Sharp Method of Turning the Tables—
Morris Recaptured, But the Other Two Free—
The Crimes for Which They
Were Held Told to Our Readers

CLARKESVILLE, Ga., February 22 [Special]

In addition to the telegram of yesterday concerning the escape of the four prisoners from Habersham jail, this much more is to say: Morris was arrested in about forty minutes after his escape by J. W. Bigham, our depot agent. He was looking for Morris and found him in a heap of brush in the woods. Bigham raised his splendid repeating rifle and ordered him to come out and surrender. He said he would, and came out, but instead of making the surrender, drew a pistol and fired at Bigham, which failed to take effect. Bigham, seeing his danger at once, shot his pistol from his hand, the ball passing through into his knee, which broke it to pieces, making amputation perhaps necessary. Mr. Bigham showed great judgment by shooting the hand which held the pistol, and by not killing him on the spot, and great courage in such a close conflict with so desperate a character. The wounds were addressed by Doctors Bun and Houston, and by night for the prisoner was placed in jail but not behind the bars for the jailer occupied that station and no key to get out. Morris said he threw the d----d key away near the railroad depot, where he was captured. Mr. John Elrod, one of the first to go in pursuit overtook the quartet near the depot but as four men were too much for him he failed to make the arrest. About twenty-five men are in search of the fugitives, and it is hoped will meet with success soon.

Besides the three murderers, Morris, Justice, and Sisk, the cattle thief negro is gone. The poor forty cent thief who is supposed to have slipped the lines, so as to perfect the escape did not leave and besides denies the charge. Mr. Groves who was hurt by trying to keep the prisoners in jail has about recovered.

THE JAILER RELEASED

The town and surroundings are greatly excited and doing all in their power to secure the escaped ones. The jailer has got out of his cage. It was found that the prisoners did not lock the doors properly, so to open them was an easy matter. It was also discovered that a hole was cut through the iron close to the lever slide. A string was placed so as to draw back the lever which was successfully carried out. Morris said that the scheme had been on foot for some time, but that they meant to wait till Mr. Groves got out before making the break. But said he, "we got mad this morning and would wait no longer, and "Morris swears fearfully while the doctors are working with his wounds."

ANOTHER STATEMENT OF THE CASE

CLARKESVILLE Ga., February 22.—[Special]

On the 21st instant, at 3 o'clock, the small son of jailer A. J. Crane came on the public street crying as to one and all to run to the jail, for the prisoners were out and his pa was locked in the jail and they had taken the key with them. A rush was made, and on entering they found all as had been stated. The jailer as usual went to get the dishes out after dinner. He ordered the prisoners into their cells and shoved back the lever which holds the cell door fasted he then entered the corridor and commenced to take up the dishes, when all at once they cell doors flew open and T. C. Justice, the murderer of J. B. Goddard, and R. H. Morris, the killer of Joseph Henderson, John A. Sisk, who killed Weston Parker, and a negro who had been stealing cattle, rushed out and secured the jailer and threw him in the back of the corridor which is in the cage. They then took the keys and passed into apartment of R. N. Graves who stopped him at the door leading out of the building, but it was only for a moment, for Morris gave him such a blow that he was obliged to let them escape. Morris had a pistol in his hand but it is not known how he got it. He aimed it at a daughter of the jailer and said:

"Don't speak, but let me out."

So they all made their way to the nearest woods which is in the direction of the Northeastern railroad. About 25 men were soon in pursuit. John Elrod was the first to overtake them. He ordered a surrender, but owing to the number and all being armed, he was obliged to retreat. By this time the sheriff, T. J. Gastly, had a full posse on the hunt. He had summoned   J. W. Bigham depot agent, to go after them with him. Bigham went, but soon discovered Morris in a brush heap near the Northeastern railroad depot. He, with his repeating rifle, drew a fine sight, and ordered a surrender. Morris said he would do so. Bigham said "Come out," but before Morris moved he fired a pistol at him and all that moment at that moment the rifle fired and Morris had a ball through his hand and into his knee.

The amputation of Morris's his leg took place during the day. Justice has been pursued by a large body of men, but to no effect. No other arrests have been made up to this hour, but the track of Justice has been found and he can't be over six miles ahead of the sheriff's party.

THE CAPTURE OF JUSTICE

Masters William Jones and Andy Gastly, son of the Sheriff, captured Justice, one of the Clarkesville jail breakers, this evening at about 5 o'clock, six miles from Tallulah. They have him there under strong guard and will bring him to Clarksville early tomorrow morning. Justice was completely lost, and was going back towards Clarkesville, traveling the public road thinking he was headed for the mountains.

MORRIS' CRIME

The prisoners were a desperate lot. Morris was convicted one year ago of the murder of Jasper Henderson and was sentenced to hang on 16 April 1886, but is now awaiting a review of his case. Jasper Henderson's wife had left him and went to the home of her mother, Mrs. Dodd. Morris deliberately borrowed a gun, went to where Henderson was, fired and killed him. The shots were from behind and thirteen buckshot entered his body. Morris claimed, in his statement that he acted in self-defense, but the evidence all showed the contrary. He told that he had killed Henderson and said he had no more regrets than if he had killed a bug. The deceased and Morris were brothers in law, having married sisters. The killing was really done on account of Henderson being charged with whipping his wife. Morris is well-connected, having been born and raised in Franklin County. He was a nephew of honorable Thomas Morris, of Carr's Hill who represented Franklin several times in the legislature, and of A. J. Morris who was at one time Ordinary of Franklin. On the trial the state introduced a number of witnesses, the principal ones being relatives of the defendant, who testified to the defendants borrowing a shotgun on the day of the tragedy, saying he was going hunting, and returning it sometime in the night, the killing having been about dusk with the remark:

"I have killed James Henderson, a damned rascal, and I don't mind it any more than if I had killed a goose."

No one saw the killing. Mrs. Ben Dodd, who was sick in her house heard the report of a gun and said that Morris came to her door and said that he had killed

James Henderson in self-defense. The testimony established his guilt beyond any doubt, the crime of being one of the darkest in the criminal history of our country. The theory of the defense was the time honored one of "self-defense;" but it rested so late on the strength of the defendant's statements, which impressed everyone as being untrue. Morris claimed that he did it in self-defense, in his statement to the court and jury he says that a few minutes before the killing he was near the house, and heard a racket up in the house between the woman and Henderson, and he ran up to see what was the matter. When he reached the scene, Henderson came at him with an axe, and asked him if he took it up, and as he came, he having his gun in hand, fired and shot him in the back.

WHY JUSTICE WAS HELD

The crime with which T. C. Justice stands charged is one of shocking brutality for the past twenty or twenty-five years a man named J. B. Goddard has lived in Towns county. Four years past he has lived in the mountains at the head of Tallulah River, near the Rabun county line. On Monday morning, January 17th, he left his home for the purpose of visiting a store across the country in Rabun. Having reached a neighbor's house, and the weather being bad, he decided to return home and go another day, and so left for his home. That was the last seen of him until the evening, when two young men of the neighborhood found him near the trail leading to his home, dead—murdered. They gave the alarm, and as soon as possible a jury was summoned and an inquest held. Suspicion soon pointed to T. C. Justice, who was found to have borrowed a gun that morning, and as the gun was found near the body. There was also appeared other evidence against him and, finally, a man who saw him commit the crime. Justice had shot his victim and then beat his head to jelly with a rock.

SISK'S SUSPICION

Sisk killed a man named Parker near Mount Airy. Sisk suspected Parker of being a revenue informer and shot him dead as he approached his house.

6 April 1887

The Atlanta Constitution (Atlanta, Georgia)

MURDER TRIAL IN TOWNS

Tilman Justice in Court for the Murder of James Goddard

Hiwassee, Ga., April 5.—[Special.]—Towns county superior court is in session this week, Judge C. J. Wellborn presiding. Besides local attorneys, W. F. Blackwell and H. C. Standridge present are: W. S. Erwin, J. J. Kinsey, W. H. Underwood, Joe Merritt, W. E. Candler, R. P. Lester and Howard Thompson, solicitor general.

The case of the state against Tilman C. Justice, charged with the offense of murdering James Goddard, an old man seventy years old, is now being tried. The state is ably represented by Howard Thompson, solicitor-general, W.F. Candler and H C. Standridge. The Defendant by J. J. Kimsey, J. W. H. Underwood and W. G. Blackwell. This is one of the most important cases ever tried in the county and has attracted a large crowd. The facts of the case are as follows:

Old man Goddard lived with his wife in the mountains east of Hiawassee, about twelve miles. One of his nearest neighbors was the defendant, Tilman C. Justice, who has a wife and several children. A feud had existed for some time between the defendant and the deceased about a road which passes through the defendant's land. This together with the fact that the defendant had been informed and believed that the deceased had reported him for violation of the internal revenue laws, and being fired with liquor is supposed to be the cause for the killing. The killing was an outrageous murder, and it is believed that the verdict of the jury will declare it and that Towns county will have a hanging.

8 April 1887

The Savannah Morning News (Savannah, Georgia)

The case of the State against Tilman C. Justice, charged with the offense of murdering James Goddard, an old man 70 years old, is now being tried in Towns county. Old man Goddard lived with his wife in the mountains east of Hiwassee, about twelve miles. One of his nearest neighbors was the defendant, Tilman S. Justice, who had a wife and several children. A feud had existed for some time between the defendant and the deceased about a road which passes through the defendant's land. This, together with the fact that the defendant had been informed and believed that the deceased had reported him for violating the internal revenue laws, and being fired with liquor, is supposed to be the cause for the killing.

7 October 1887

The Macon Telegraph (Macon, Georgia)

TO BE HANGED

Clarksville Advertiser.

At towns county Superior Court last week, Tillman Justice was convicted of the murder of James B. Goddard in Towns county sometime last winter, and sentenced to be hanged on the 18th day of November next. Mr. R. P. Burch, the gentlemanly and excellent sheriff of Towns accompanied by a small posse in charge of the condemned man, spent Friday night in Clarksville, and on Saturday morning Mr. Burch proceeded with him to Gainesville, where he is to be confined to await the day of his execution.

9 November 1887

The Atlanta Constitution (Atlanta, Georgia)

THE GOVERNOR AND HIS CABINET

THE GOVERNOR HAS refused to commute the sentence of Tillman C. Justice, convicted of the murder of John (sic) Goddard at the September term, 1887, of Town's superior court, and sentenced to be hanged on November 18, 1887.

A very lengthy petition was presented by Hon. J. M. Bleckley, Chief Justice Bleckley's brother, to commute the sentence to imprisonment for life. The governor declined to commute the sentence on the ground that the testimony showed that the offense was murder. Justice killed Goddard because he was supposed to have given information to revenue officials.

9 November 1887

The Macon Telegraph (Macon, Georgia)

HE MUST DIE.

The Governor Refuses to Interpose Between Justice and the Halter.

ATLANTA, November 8.—In the Superior Court of Towns County, September 20, 1887, Tillman C. Justice was convicted of the murder of James B. Goddard, and sentenced to be hanged on the 18th of the present month. Tillman killed Goddard, an old man, because he believed Goddard had informed on him to the revenue officials.

An application for a commutation of the sentence to life imprisonment has been pending before the Governor for some days. The petition was an unusually long one. The governor to-day refused to interfere for the reason that the evidence showed the crime to be a brutal murder, and left no doubt whatever as to the guilt of Justice.

19 November 1887

The Macon Telegraph (Macon, Georgia)

FRIDAY'S FATAL DROP.

TILLMAN JUSTICE EXECUTED
AT HIWASSEE, TOWNS COUNTY.

Particulars of the Atrocious Murder of
Old Man Goddard for Which Justice was Hanged—
The Efforts to Secure Commutation.

ATLANTA, November 18.—Tillman Justice was hung at Hiwassee, Towns County today for the murder of James B. Goddard.

The crime was a particularly brutal one.

Justice was a one-armed man in the neighborhood of fifty years of age. He belonged to that apparently numerous class in North Georgia counties called "moonshiners."

Goddard was an old man who lived in the neighborhood, and had for some time been

SUSPECTED OF BEING AN INFORMER. Previous to the murder Justice had, upon one occasion, remarked that Goddard had better attend to his own business, and not concern himself with the affairs of other people.

Finally, last winter, Justice determined to get rid of the man he believed to be an informer, and went at his purpose in a very deliberate and cold blooded way. Early one morning, cold, with snow all over the country, he waylaid his unsuspecting victim in a country road, and fired upon him with a shotgun.

GODDARD FELL TO THE GROUND. The wound was not fatal, and the wounded man crawled into the woods, and, fearing another attack, hid under a brush.

Later his assailant followed and the bloody track to where the wounded man was concealed, and finding him still alive beat him in the head with a heavy rock until breath and life were gone out of the old man.

There was some excitement over the murder at the time, and when Justice was arrested he was carried to Gainesville for safe keeping,

At the spring term of the Towns Superior Court, Judge Wellborn presiding

JUSTICE WAS CONVICTED of the crime and sentenced to be hung today.

Justice was carried back to the Gainesville jail where he was confined until a few days ago, when the sheriff of Towns county took him to Hiwassee for execution.

During the stay of Justice in the Gainesville jail, he professed religion, and announced that he was ready to go.

Some weeks ago an effort was made to induce Governor to commute the sentence to life imprisonment. This application was personally made and urged by Mr. Frank A Bleckley, a brother of the chief justice.

HIS ARGUMENT before the Governor was that Justice was convicted on circumstantial evidence, and that the principal witness was a very unreliable one, whose credit had been impeached, and who was strongly suspected of being an accomplice of Justice.

On these grounds Mr. Bleckley thought the sentence should be commuted. The Governor took a different view. The evidence left no doubt as to the guilt of the man and the brutality of the crime made executive clemency out of the question.

THE EXECUTION was public, and was witnessed by a large concourse of people. Justice manifested considerable fortitude to the last and died after a few spasmodic struggles. When cut done it was found that the drop had done its work well and that the neck was broken by the fall.

18 November 1887

The Evening World, (New York, New York)

JUSTICE THE MOONSHINER, HANGED.

[SPECIAL TO THE WORLD.]

CANTON, Ga., Nov. 18—Tillman C. Justice was hanged at Hiawassee at noon to-day. Several hundred people witnessed the execution. The trap was sprung by Sheriff W. D. Burch. Justice was an illicit distiller. James B. Goddard, his neighbor, was opposed to moonshiners and was suspected of having reported several illicit stills. Justice shot him down one day while passing his house and then brained him with the butt of his gun. Justice was aged thirty and Goddard seventy-five.

19 November 1887

The Morning News, (Savannah, Georgia)

A HANGING IN TOWNS

The Brutal Murderer of an Old Man Pays the Penalty

ATLANTA, Ga., Nov, 18 – Tillman C. Justice was hanged in Towns county today for the murder of J. B. Goddard.

Justice spent his confinement at Gainesville where he professed religion, and said he was willing to die. The Governor was asked to commute his sentence. The application was urged by Frank A. Bleckley of Clayton, brother of the Chief Justice, but the Governor declined to intervene.

HISTORY OF THE CRIME

On Jan 14, 1887, James B. Goddard, an old and respectable man of Towns county was found dead in the woods near a path where he usually walked between his house and one of his neighbors, where he had been the morning before his death. Circumstances pointed to the defendant in this case and he was arrested. An investigation showed that Mr. Goddard had been shot in the face with a shotgun, and then it was plain that his head was beaten up with a long rock which was found by his side. The evidence showed that Tillman C. Justice had made threats at various times that he was going to kill the old man and the morning of the day that Goddard was found dead, that Justice went to a man by the name of Rodgers and borrowed a shotgun, stating he wanted to kill some turkeys, and, after securing the gun, he went off down the path upon which the old man was found. In a short time the report of the gun attracted the attention of the neighbor, and knowing that Justice had made the threat to kill the old man (Goddard), he was alarmed, and sent two of his sons, telling them that he was afraid that Justice had met the old man down there and had killed him. The boys went immediately, and found the deceased, as above stated. Then it was further shown that Justice went to a place nearby where two young men were working, and told them he had shot one of the d----- biggest sheep that they had ever seen up there, pointing in the direction of the place of the crime. He got down on his knees and showed the men how the old man prayed and begged him. Near the body was found the gun that Justice borrowed, stuck under a log. From all the circumstances in the case, the jury found Justice guilty of murder. The trouble between the men, which was supposed to be the cause of the murder, was that Justice was thought to be running a distillery in the neighborhood, and Mr. Goddard seemed to be opposed to such violation of the law. He had made some remarks about it and stated that he wished he knew who to write to and report the still. After the verdict of guilty was found Justice confessed the crime, but implicated one of the principle witnesses as being an accomplice in the murder, as he had an interest in the still and helped to plan the murder.

22 November 1887

The Weekly Constitution (Atlanta, Georgia)

BY THE NECK.

The Hanging of Tillman C. Justice in Towns County.

A DASTARDLY CRIME AVENGED

GAINESVILLE, Ga., November 18.—[Special.]

Tillman C. Justice, the murderer of James B. Goddard, was hanged today in Hiwassee, Towns county.

A brief history of his trouble with Mr. Goddard and of his crime in finally murdering him, is as follows:

Justice was a moonshiner, and was running a rented still in the wilds of Towns county. In his employee was a young man by the name of Coward, a son of Jason Coward, who was the only eye-witness to the horrible crime. Goddard and Justice were adjoining land owners, and lived one mile from each other. While they were close neighbors, peace did not reign between them, but on frequent occasions they had their differences about land lines and other matters. Jason Coward, who is a conspicuous figure in the commission of the crime as stated by the condemned man, lived about eight miles from Justice, and on Sunday evening before the killing on Monday, came to the house of Justice to inform him and his son, young Coward, that old man Goddard had reported the still, saying that Goddard ought to be killed. Young Coward was at the still house and did not see his father at Justice's house, but saw him as he passed the still on his way to the house of Colonel Rodgers, where he spent the night. At supper on Sunday night young Coward told Justice that he had seen his father, and that he had told him that old man Goddard had reported the still and that they were likely to get into trouble about it. Young Coward after supper returned to his post at the still, and on Monday morning while Justice was sleeping, Jason Coward was knocking at his door for admittance. He was admitted and the two began drinking whisky to prepare them for the tragedy.

The story of the murder, as told by the doomed man is as follows:

During the morning Coward saw old man Goddard pass the house in the big road, which was about one hundred yards from the house, and called to Justice. They then decided to load Justice's double barreled shot gun, and lying patiently for his return. Coward charged both barrels heavily with small shot. For two hours they sat upon the piazza with their eyes strained in the direction from whence Goddard would come, and ever and anon taking draught of the poisonous fire-water.

While thus engaged and at the height of their revels, old man Goddard made his appearance, and now was their time for action.

In a twinkling they were in line on the march to carry out their premeditated murder. They walked briskly for three quarters of a mile and in a quarter of the victim's home, where they halted and again waited to see the old man. Goddard had reached his three score years, and his step was slow and feeble, but on and on he came, innocent of danger and of the dreadful fate which awaited him. He turned out of the road into a trail, and kept moving toward his home—he looked up and in ten steps to the front and in the trail stood the two men, one with a gun pointing toward him Justice, who held the gun charged him with reporting his still. He replied:

"I did not do it."

Justice pulled the trigger and the charge took effect in Goddard's face: again Justice pulled the trigger and the charge broke Goddard's arm. Not satisfied, Justice advanced upon Goddard, and made an effort to brain him with the gun, but the gun hit a log over Goddard's head and was snapped at the lock plate, and the locks and barrels fell to the ground, and his work was done. Justice dashed the butt down, and at once Coward picked up the barrels and butt, and carried them a distance of one hundred and sixty yards, where he hid them under the side of a log covering them with leaves. Old man Goddard was left upon the ground as he fell, weltering in his blood and the demons hastening away made an effort to hid their awful crime.

Jason Coward went over to Hightower creek that evening and told Davis Burl that Justice had killed old man Goddard. The body of the murdered man was found that evening and a large crowd was assembled when the killing was announced in the settlement. Justice was among the crowd but kept his secret, and Coward did not make his appearance until the next day. The locks of the gun were found on the evening of the day of the murder, where they had been left, and on the next morning the butt and barrels were brought out from their hiding place.

Justice was arrested and charged with the commission of the crime, and at the March term, 1887, the Towns superior court, he was tried for the murder, but a mistrial was declared, the jury standing eleven for conviction and one for acquittal. He was placed in the Hall county jail for safe keeping, and on the 2nd day of June, he, together with G. V. Ayers, the safe blowers, and two negroes made their escape; but Justice and Ayers were captured in Habersham county on or about the 7th of June, and again placed in Jail in Gainesville.

At the September term of Towns superior court he was again called to answer to the indictment for murder, and he answered "Not guilty." The prosecution was conducted by Solicitor General Howard Thompson, who was assisted by H. C. Standridge, of Hiawassee, while the defense was in the hands of John. J. Kimsey, of Cleveland, and W. G. Blackwell of Hiawassee. After a trial lasting two days Justice was found guilty of murder in the first degree, and his honor C. J. Wellborn, sentenced him to be hung on the 18th day of November. Justice and the judge lived in adjoining counties, and were acquaintances, and the judge was moved to tears while passing the sentence of death upon the doomed man. The gun was recognized as Justice's gun, and this was strong evidence against him. Justice was about thirty years of age, and has a wife and three children, five three and two years of age, whom he leaves in destitute circumstances as he gave his property to his counsel for defending him. He was born and reared in Raybun county, and was a quiet and unassuming man until he commenced to still and drink, when he became hardened. Goddard left a wife about forty-five years of age, without any children and left good property for that section of the country.

Justice spent the most of his time, after his sentence in reading the Bible and making ready for the conclusion of the whole matter. He was quite anxious for ministers to visit him and assist him in making peace with his God.

12 *January 1888*

Sioux City Journal (Sioux City, Iowa)

A GEORGIA SENSATION

Hanged and Resuscitated

Gainesville, GA., Jan. 11.—For a week rumors have been coming into this city that Tillman C. Justice, baring a slight crick in the neck, was alive and well in his mountain home. To-Day a gentleman arrived from Towns count who gives positive assurance that the hanging of Justice was a sham; that his body was quickly cut down and was resuscitated, and that a dozen men in Hiwassee have conversed with him since the fatal 19th of November, upon which day he was supposed to have been executed.

Tillman C. Justice was an illicit distiller in Towns county, had for a neighbor John (sic) B. Goddard, a retired lawyer aged 72. Goddard was suspected of giving the revenue officials information concerning the moonshiners, and as for this reason he was shot dead by Justice. The murderer was kept in the jail of this city awaiting his execution and when the date arrived was carried to that county. Towns county is high up in the mountains, sixty miles away from the nearest railway station, and is so cut off that its existence is not known to most people. It is overrun by moonshiners and therefore it would be an easy matter for friendly officers to save a friend. The editor of the Dahlonega Signal is authority for the statement the a breathing motion was noticed in the breast of Justice when he was cut down. Certain it is that the belief of Justice having escaped with his live is strong and general.

12 January 1888

The Weekly News Democrat (Emporia, Kansas)

TILLMAN C. JUSTICE, A MOONSHINER, HANGED FOR MURDER

CUT DOWN BY FRIENDS WHILE ALIVE AND RESUSCITATED

SHAM HANGING

Gainesville, GA., Jan 10—Yesterday a gentleman from Towns County gave positive assurance that the hanging of Tillman C. Justice was a sham; that his body was quickly cut down and resuscitated, and that a dozen men in Hiwassee have conversed with him since November 19 when he was supposed to have been hanged. Justice was an illicit distiller in Towns county. John (sic) B. Goddard, a retired lawyer aged seventy-two, was suspected of giving revenue officials information concerning moonshiners and for this reason he was shot dead by Justice. The place of execution was remote from civilization, surrounded by Justice's friends and it was an easy matter for friendly officers to save a friend. The editor of the Sahlonega (sic) Signal is authority for the statement that justice was still alive when he was cut down.

17 January 1888

The Weekly Public Ledger (Memphis, Tennessee)

JUSTICE'S JOB

**Poorly Executed—He is Cut Down
from the Gallows and Resuscitated.**

New York, January 10.—A Gainesville (Ga.) special says: For a week rumors have been coming into this city that Tillman C. Justice, barring a slight soreness in his neck, was alive and well in his mountain home. Yesterday a gentleman arrived from Towns count, who gives positive assurance that the hanging of Justice was a sham; that his body was quickly cut down and resuscitated, and that a dozen men in Hiawassee conversed with him on November 19th, when he was supposed to have been hanged. Justice was an illicit distiller in Towns county who had for a neighbor John (sic) B. Goddard, a retired lawyer aged seventy-two. Goddard was suspected of giving the revenue officials information concerning the moonshiners, and for this reason he was shot dead by Justice. The murderer was kept in the jail of this city awaiting his hanging, and when the date arrived was carried to that county. Town county is high up in the mountains, sixty miles away from the nearest railway station, and it is so cut off that its existence is not known to most people. It is overrun by moonshiners, and, therefore it would be an easy matter for friendly officers to save a friend. The editor the Dahlonega Signal is authority for the statement that Justice was still breathing when he was cut down.

20 January 1888

The Ivanhoe Times (Ivanhoe, Kansas)

It is declared that Tillman Justice, the illicit distiller who killed a U. S. Marshall and was hanged at Gainesville, Georgia, is yet alive, having been quickly cut down and resuscitated.

27 January 1888

The Constitution (Atlanta, Georgia)

TILMAN C. JUSTICE IS CERTAINLY DEAD

BLAIRSVILLE, Ga., January 22, Editor's Constitution: The report going the rounds of the press to the effect that Tilman C. Justice, who was hung in Hiawassee, Towns county, Ga., last year for the murder of James Godard, is not dead but is still living is a great injustice to one of the best sheriffs in the state and a gross reflection on the official character of Sheriff Burch, who knows no such words as fail in the discharge of duty however hard it may be. Justice is certainly dead, dead, dead, and it is to be hoped that the Lord had mercy on his soul. The Judgement of the court was fully satisfied.

W. E. CANDLER

5 February 1888

The Atlanta Constitution (Atlanta, Georgia)

JUSTICE IS DEAD

That is, Tillman C. Justice, of Towns County, North Carolina (sic)

Werne, N.C., January 29, 1888.—Editors Constitution: Noticing in your weekly edition an article headed "A Strange Story" and crediting same to Dahlonega Signal, I think perhaps the best means of answering the same to write direct to your paper, requesting you to give it place in your weekly edition. I have received marked copies of Detroit Free Press, Grand Rapids, Michigan, Democrat and Jackson County, Ga., Herald containing references to the same story, as well as numerous private inquiries. Regarding the alleged living of Tillman C. Justice, I can say this much. He was hanged November 18th last. He dropped between five and six feet, hung suspended by the neck without a struggle excepting two heavings of the chest for a period of twenty-four minutes by my watch. Was examined and pronounced dead by Drs. W. H. McClure and Robert Twiggs, of Hiwassee, Ga., and Drs. D. W. Killian and B. G. Webb of Hayesville, N. C., Dr. Medford Meese of Pigeon River, N.C., and Dr. William Haynes of Franklin, N. C., and myself. After being cut down, he was placed in the coffin and the physicians present removed the cap and examined him thoroughly, pronouncing him dead from a broken neck. Probably consumed twenty minutes in such examination. All these movements being performed in open air and with bright daylight before an audience of one thousand to fifteen hundred people, perhaps. So much I am knowing to personally. Regarding subsequent events, there is no question as to his final disposition. He was taken to the residence of T. C. Allen and there was kept overnight, and in the morning I am informed a post mortem examination was made. Be that as it may, he was buried on Sunday, before at least three hundred people. After death and removal of cap, his face was found black and black line around the neck where the rope touched. There was not the shadow of a doubt as to death among any of the physicians present. The Gainesville dispatch says "We are away up in the mountains, and so far removed from civilization," that we could not be expected to possess much knowledge. But I want to say that as physicians. I think all of us could tell whether a man was dead or not, under such circumstances, in forty or forty-five minutes of steady examination. I have avoided the use of technical terms for the benefit of the "uncivilized" portion of your readers, for whom this is particularly intended. Another item in the Gainesville dispatch says towns count is overrun with moonshiners. Such is not the case. I practice medicine over a large portion of this county, and I don't think there is a single still in operation, moonshine or otherwise.

Very Truly, GEORGE T. HINE. M.D., Werne N. C.

15 July 1942

The Atlanta Constitution (Atlanta, Georgia)

DUDLEY GLASS

Good Old Days

Bit of rural Georgia history is found in T. J. Lance's column in the Towns County Herald: "I asked Jule Twiggs what is the biggest murder trial in the history of the county and this was his answer: It was the case of Tillman Justice who killed a man by the name of Goddard. The first trial was a mistrial but in the next term of the court he was convicted and sentenced to hang."

"The date of the hanging was fixed for November 18, 1887. (sic) Mr. Twiggs says that he remembers the incidents and that he was present himself. He said that five to seven thousand people from as far away as 50 miles came to the hanging. Big Pense Burch was the county sheriff. The rope that was used in the hanging was cut into small pieces and given (to) the people who wanted to keep them as souvenirs of the hanging. Mr. Twiggs says further that this was the only murder case that brought the death penalty in the whole history of the county."

25 April 2018

The Towns County Herald (Hiawassee, Georgia) Used with permission.

Taylor Recounts Hanging at Historical Society Meeting

By Mark Novak
Towns County Herald Staff Writer

Bad blood resulted in the death of two Towns County men in the late 1800s, and County Historian Jerry Taylor told the tale in the April 9 meeting of the Towns County historical Society.

The year was 1887, and Tillman C. Justice was a local resident with something to hide—he knew if word got out, he would be in trouble with the law. Justice was a moonshiner and ran a still on his property and he aimed to protect his interests in the moonshine business.

Backing up just a bit from '87, U. S. Congress created the Internal Revenue Service to collect taxes on liquor, tobacco, and other items during the War Between the States. And though it was not illegal at the time to operate a still, it was illegal not to pay taxes on the ill-gotten gains. Many Georgians at the time refused to pay taxes on the liquor they produced and kept their stills well hidden from the government, much like Justice in 1887.

Enter James B. Godard.

Godard owned property next to Justice, and the two argued over property lines for years, creating animosity between the men. Another man named Jason Coward told his son David, who worked the still with Justice, that Godard had reported the still. He also told his son that Godard ought to be killed for it. Young Coward soon after informed Justice over dinner just what his father had told him, before returning to his post at the still.

The very next day, the elder Coward and Justice began to drink heartily in preparation for the coming crime. The men loaded Justice's double-barreled shot gun and laid in wait for Godard to come by, all the while drinking more and more whiskey. Finally, Godard appeared at his home, and the two confronted him about reporting the still.   Godard denied reporting the still, but Justice didn't believe him. He pulled the trigger and hit Godard in the face then shot him a second time and broke his arm.

Well, Coward reported the murder that evening, and the body was found as well as the gun used in the murder. Justice was charged with the murder and the trial was held in Towns Count, ending in a mistrial with the jury being 11 for conviction and one for acquittal. Justice was held in jail to be retried.

Justice escaped jail with three other prisoners, only to be caught five days later, and he was called again to answer the charge for murder. This time, he was convicted and sentenced to hanging on November 18, 1887, for murder in the first degree.

Taylor relied upon an 1887 article from the Atlanta Constitution for retelling the only hanging in Towns County history.

25 November 2020

The Towns County Herald (Hiawassee, Georgia)

Used with permission.

PAST & PRESENT

Jerry Taylor

A Day When the Past Connected to the Present

The crudely hand-carved stone in remote secluded Old Smyrna Cemetery on Charlie's Creek reads, "SACRED TO THE MEMORY OF J. B. GODARD WAS BORN SEPT. 18 AD 1818. DEPARTED THIS LIFE BY BEING MURDERED JAN. 17 AD 1887." For one-hundred and thirty-three years, the stone has stood as a silent sentinel of Godard's grave. In all that time, no descendant has been to visit his final resting place. That was until Saturday November 21, when members of the Towns County Historical Society escorted his third great grandson to the old cemetery.

Mr. Godard was among Towns County's earliest settlers and made his living as a lawyer and proprietor of a tippling house in Hiawassee before being brutally murdered on the Charlie's Creek Road by Tilmon C. Justice in 1887. The established motive for the murder was that Mr. Godard had reported Mr. Justice to the authorities for illicit distilling. Mr. Justice was convicted of the murder at the September term of Towns County Superior Court and was sentenced by Judge C. J. Wellborn to be hanged on November 18, 1887.

Earlier this year, Dr. William Thomas of Augusta, Georgia found the memorial of his great-great-great grandfather, James B. Godard on findagrave.com. Keenly interested in his family history and wanting to find out as much as possible about his connection with Towns County, Dr. Thomas contacted Sandra Green, president of the Towns County Historical Society who put him in touch with County Historian Jerry Taylor and Steve Eller who mounted an effort to clean and restore Old Smyrna Cemetery.

Soon, Jerry Taylor organized a local effort to take Dr. Thomas to visit his ancestor's final resting place, which took place on November 21, 2020. It was a bone-rattling ride on Charlie's Creek Road to reach the destination. Following the cemetery visit and before returning to Hiawassee, the group explored the highland area by visiting the Old Smyrna Church site on Flat Branch, Charlie's Creek, Tallulah River, Tate City, and Persimmon.

Towns County Historical Society Members who took part in the trip and tour of the area were Sandra Green, president; Jerry Taylor, vice-president and County Historian; Steve and Jan Eller, Smyrna Cemetery project leaders, Jesse Cook, former game warden who is familiar with the area; and Bruce Roberts who has logged many steps in the high country and is familiar with the territory and flora of the area.

As a side note, Steve Eller's interest in Old Smyrna Cemetery comes from the fact that it is also the final resting place of his ancestor Hardy Washington Eller (1843-1908) who served on the jury that convicted Tilmon C. Justice in the murder of James B. Godard. Another interesting connection is that Sandra Green is a direct descendant of the namesake of Charlie's Creek, Charles B. "Charlie" Rogers, whose gun was used by Tilmon C. Justice to murder James B. Godard.

November 21, 2020 was an awesome day when the past connected with the present.

Acknowledgements

First, I must thank my wife and best friend, Paula, for her patience and encouragement as I worked on this second project. Thanks also to my manuscript reviewers, all of whom provided great inputs—Mary Rae Dudley, William Greenleaf, Sarah Frances Munzenrider, Jim and Renee Neiman, Keenan and Lisa Templeton, Allen Edmunds, Cynthia Bennett, Josephine Neill Browning, Megan Arrington, and Michele Herfurth. Thank you so much for your time, encouragement, and support!

About The Author

William Thomas follows up his debut novel with another gripping story—this time from his own family's history. Interesting anecdotes about an ancestor had been whispered at family reunions, but the full picture didn't come to light until the author met a Georgia historian who knew a great deal more. They pieced together the ignominious path of a man that ended with a brutal murder and made newspaper headlines across the nation in 1887.

After graduating from Ole Miss in 1987 and the University of Mississippi School of Medicine in 1991, Dr. Thomas finished a career in the U.S. Air Force as an Internal Medicine Physician, Flight Surgeon, and Commander.

His first novel, *Runaway Haley*, was the recipient of the 2021 John Esten Cook Award for Southern fiction. He lives in Georgia with his wife, Paula, where he still practices medicine.

AVAILABLE FROM GREEN ALTAR BOOKS

If you enjoyed this book, perhaps some of our other titles will pique your interest. The following titles are now available for your reading pleasure…

Enjoy!

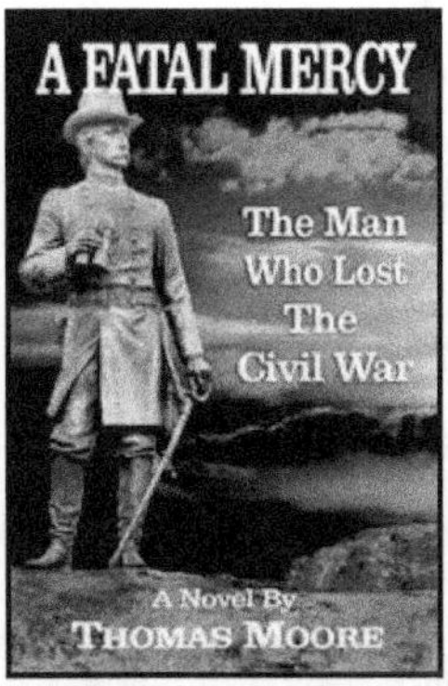

GREEN ALTAR BOOKS
SHOTWELL PUBLISHING

Green Altar (Literary Imprint)

CATHARINE BROSMAN

An Aesthetic Education and Other Stories (2nd Ed)

Chained Tree, Chained Owls: Poems

Aerosols and Other Poems

RANDALL IVEY

A New England Romance:
And Other Southern Stories

JAMES E. KIBBLER, JR.

Tiller : Clayback County Series, Vol. 4

THOMAS MOORE

A Fatal Mercy: The Man Who Lost The Civil War

PERRIN LOVETT

The Substitute, Tom Ironsides 1

KAREN STOKES

Belles

Carolina Love Letters

Carolina Twilight

Honor in the Dust

The Immortals

The Soldier's Ghost: A Tale of Charleston

WILLIAM THOMAS

Runaway Haley: An Imagined Family Saga

Gold-Bug
(Mystery & Suspense Imprint)

BRANDI PERRY

Splintered: A New Orleans Tale

MARTIN WILSON

To Jekyll and Hide